CHRISTIAN

D1488000

"Freshman?"

"Yeah, how could you tell?"

"It's easy . . ."

"You're a big boy now," Kandi chided. "You're in college, you know, not kindergarten!"

Rick was beginning to wish he had stayed at the dorm—but how could he get away from the party now?

Finally, he excused himself, went out and started running . . .

Boyd County Public Library

Kent County Public Library

THE
FRESHMAN

THE FRESHMAN

Ed L. Groenhoff

ACCENT BOOKS

Denver, Colorado

F
GRO

ACCENT BOOKS

A division of Accent Publications, Inc.
12100 W. Sixth Avenue
P.O. Box 15337
Denver, Colorado 80215

Copyright©1983 Accent Publications, Inc.
Printed in the United States of America

All rights reserved. No portion of this book may be reproduced
in any form without the written permission of the publishers,
with the exception of brief excerpts in magazine reviews.

Library of Congress Catalog Card Number 83-71507
ISBN 0-89636-110-1

First Printing 1983

Second Printing 1984

1.15.96 gift 6.99 c.1

To
Wayne and Kevin,
who keep me thinking young

Contents

1/ Good-bye and Hello 11

2/ Friday Night in Mill City 25

3/ The Morning After 35

4/ Emancipation 47

5/ The Party 55

6/ Blue Monday 65

7/ Psych Class 75

8/ A Crusade 83

9/ Dinner at Leonard's 93

10/ Going Home 103

11/ Another Party 115

12/ Exit—Stage Left 125

13/ Where is Home? 137

14/ Coming Home 145

Good-bye and Hello

A tractor, pulling a piece of farm machinery, suddenly appeared on the narrow two-lane highway, bringing Rick back to the reality of the road.

"Why don't they stay in the fields where they belong?" he muttered to himself.

At the first opportunity, Rick slammed the accelerator to the floor and sped around the tractor, glaring at the driver as he did so.

"There goes another quart," he thought, as he glanced in the rearview mirror and saw a cloud of smoke trailing his '76 Plymouth. It was beginning to take a quart of oil with every tank of gas, and sudden acceleration like this didn't help the situation.

Except for these interruptions, Rick's mind was far from the southern Minnesota countryside. A thousand thoughts were clamoring for his attention today, and most of the time he was driving with his mind set on automatic pilot.

Now and then a vivid image or a distinct sound came into sharp focus, but most of the time his thoughts came and went in a wild jumble, resulting in a blurred, noisy daydream. Rick hadn't slept much in the past 24 hours, so both mental and physical fatigue were hindering clear thinking.

Snatches of the previous night kept coming back. "Sure wish you didn't have to go," Ann had said, trying to hold back her tears.

"Yeah, me too," Rick had replied. "I've been looking forward to the day I could leave home and go to college ever since I was in the ninth grade . . . and now, well, now that day is here, and I'm not so sure about it."

"Why couldn't summer have lasted forever?" Ann had said in a dreamy voice.

"If the summer hadn't been so great, it would be a lot easier to go," Rick had replied.

There had always been plenty of girls willing to date and Rick had made the most of the situation.

"I love 'em all," Rick had told his envious friends, "and I'm much too smart to let one of them tie me down."

But the summer had changed all of that. With a little planning, and some providential help, Rick and Ann had both applied, and were accepted for the work crew at a Bible camp. So during part of June and all of July and August, they had spent all of their free time together. During the summer their relationship had deepened, and last night everything seemed to fall into place.

There had been dinner with the family, and then a farewell party at church, so it was well past midnight before Rick and Ann were finally alone. He had driven to their favorite spot in Wirth park. Ann moved closer, and Rick slipped his arm around her.

Those last moments together were entirely different than either of them had envisioned. There was none of that nonsensical chatter which had characterized so many other evenings together. They were very serious, and suddenly they both felt very grown-up.

"What do you plan to do in life?" Ann had asked.

"I'm not really sure," Rick had answered honestly. "I think I would like to go into business, but I guess I'll just have to take some general courses at first and maybe I will find something I like."

"You plan to get married, don't you?" Ann asked.

"Sure," Rick answered, "doesn't everyone?"

"Suppose so," Ann said, "but some seem to be in a bigger rush than others."

"You in a rush?" Rick asked.

"Not particularly."

"Could you wait until I get through college?" Rick asked.

There was a pause while Ann was obviously choosing her words carefully. Finally she pressed her body even tighter against his and said, "Right now I'm ready to wait forever if that's what it takes to get you."

They sat quietly for a long time. Rick felt the warm body next to his and wished he could hold her there forever. He had never experienced anything quite like this before. It was like saying "hello" and "good-bye" at the same time, and when the final "good-bye" did come, it was devastating for both of them.

Now as the miles rolled by, other bits of last night came into focus. There was a conversation with Dr. Kenley, who had been invited to the party too. Kenley had made a point of talking to Rick alone.

"Be true to your commitment to God, Rick, and remember, we'll be praying for you," he had said.

Rick stuck out his hand, feeling a little embarrassed, but managing an innocent grin. "Sure, Dr. Kenley, don't worry about me. Thanks for everything."

Now Rick's thoughts shifted from the past to the future. He wondered what dorm life would be like. Who would be his roommate? Would he be able to do the work? After all, he hadn't exactly been the best student in his high school class.

And then he thought about his parents. It was their money that was sending him to college. He had saved some from the summer job, but it didn't even begin to pay for the first quarter's tuition. He was suddenly struck by how much this was costing his parents. He felt in his shirt pocket to see if his checkbook was still there.

"This should take care of the first quarter's tuition," his dad had said, handing him a deposit slip that morning. "You'll have to pay for your own books, but let me know what the dorm bill is, and I'll send you the money for that."

His parents loved him. He knew that, but they hadn't been much help in preparing him for college. Both had gone to trade schools directly out of high school and were married and working full-time jobs before they were twenty.

His mother had talked about going back to school, but instead, began to raise a family. First came Rick, and then Heather, and finally Bill. After that she went back to work to help pay the expenses of a growing family. She had given up the idea of going back to school, but she was determined that her children would have a college education.

Rick had selected Southern for several reasons. For one thing, the tuition was less than at either the State University or any of the private colleges which he had checked. And since it was almost 200 miles from home, he figured he would do more studying and be less involved with activities around home and church. Also Southern had around ten thousand students, which, he thought, was just about the right size. It wasn't so big that it would be totally impersonal, yet it was big enough to offer a variety of majors.

It was mid-afternoon when Rick pulled up before the dorm which had been assigned to him.

"So this is home?" he muttered out loud. The thought gave him a feeling of nausea, and it was several minutes before he could make himself get out of the car.

Rick found the front desk and presented his letter of admission. The fellow on duty, obviously an upperclassman, gave him a key to his assigned room, and pointed the way to the nearest stairs.

The room was just as it had been pictured in the college catalog. It was about 12 by 14 feet with a large picture window at one end. On either side of the room were single beds with built-in desks. At the foot of the beds, near the door, were built-in dressers and closets.

His roommate obviously hadn't arrived, and the room seemed empty and uninviting. A combination of fear of the unknown, and the emotional and physical stress of the previous twenty-four hours began to get to Rick, and he felt the lump in his stomach growing larger by the minute. He had a faint memory of having felt this way once before. He sat down on the bed, and put his head in his hands. The memory became more vivid, and he could see his parents' car as it went down a tree-lined road, leaving him at a summer camp for the first time. He was only nine years old when that took place, but it still hurt whenever he thought about it.

Rick lifted his head, and saw himself in the full-length mirror which was attached to the back side of the closet door. He stood up, walked over to the mirror, and began to examine himself. He looked up and down his image very slowly as if viewing a total stranger. It occured to him that he hadn't taken time to really look at himself for a long time.

What he saw was a well-proportioned, 5 foot 9 inch body, weighing 152 lbs. His naturally blond hair was almost white—the product of the summer's sun. He was wearing a white knit T-shirt, faded cut-offs, and white sweat socks. The contrast between the white clothes and the dark skin made him look almost bronze. Swimming and working at camp had kept him in good physical condition, and although he was no muscleman, he knew that a walk on the beach was always good for a few stares from the girls.

The man which Rick saw in the mirror didn't match the childish, homesick feeling which was deep inside. Finally, he looked himself squarely in the eyes and said, "Come on, Rick, this is college, not kindergarten. You can do it!"

Rick had just brought the last box in from the car when he heard a voice say, "This your room?"

He turned around to see another fellow standing in the doorway. He was about Rick's height, but more muscular, and with a mass of tangled red hair outlining a freckled face.

"Guess so," Rick answered.

"Mine too," the stranger said, coming into the room. "Guess we're roommates."

"Must be," Rick responded, his voice showing a lack of enthusiasm.

"What's your name?" the other fellow said, looking around the room.

"Rick. Rick Erickson. What's yours?"

"Bert Kemp," he answered, dropping his full weight into one of the armchairs, and pulling out a cigarette.

"If we're going to live together, you might as well know something about me," Bert began, striking a match.

"I'm from the Cities, and I came here for one reason—to get away from home. I'm in college because my old man sent me, or I'd be hitting the road for somewhere. Should be a sophomore this year, but flunked a couple courses last year. Even got kicked off the hockey team because I couldn't hack Math."

Bert took a long draw on the cigarette, and continued without waiting for a comment from Rick. "This is a real party school, you know. Did I have fun last year! And I'm looking forward to more of the same this year. By the way, why are you here?"

Rick realized he was staring at Bert, and blushed. "Well, I'm not sure. My high school counselor told me I had the right interests for business, but I don't know if I can make the grade."

"The head shrinker at school called me in one time and showed me the results of one of those interest tests," Bert said. "Know what it showed? Said that I could be a mortician. Can you imagine that? Bert, the friendly undertaker!"

Bert thought this was extremely funny, and laughed so loudly that his voice echoed up and down the empty halls. He got up to look for an ash tray, and saw Rick's keys lying on his desk. "Hey, I lucked out—a roommate with a car! What you got?"

"It's only a '76 Plymouth," Rick answered. "Completely stock, and as stripped down as they come. Bought it last year from another kid at school."

"Quit complaining. I've only got a '74 Chev. and I wrecked it last week. After the accident, the old man got sore and wouldn't let me bring it to school. I'll talk him into it next quarter."

A thin, tall boy, with pointed nose and chin, and black wavy hair came into the room. "So this is your hole, Bert. It already smells like you. This your roommate?"

"Yeah, this is my cell mate. Rick, meet Paul, a buddy of mine from high school."

"Hi, Paul," Rick said, sticking out his hand.

"Glad to meet you, Rick. I pity you having to live with this mug. I did last year, so I know all about it. If you want to know anything about him, just ask me. I've known him since grade school, so I know his record. And believe me, he has a record! Let's see. At last count, he has had three speeding tickets, one overnight in jail for a fight, one open bottle arrest . . ."

"Aw, come off it," Bert laughed. "Your record is long-playing too. Just wait till I play it for Rick."

"How about getting your things out of my car first?" Paul said. "I've got a date tonight, you know."

"How's that for making time? He hasn't unpacked yet, and already he's thinking about women. Of course, we aren't as unfortunate as Paul. He had to bring his woman along. We're free to do what we want, aren't we, Rick?" Bert said, winking at Rick.

"Poor old Paul," Bert continued. "His girl decided to come to school with him. She just didn't trust him with all these college women."

Bert put out his cigarette and slapped Paul on the back. "O.K., old man, let's unload that crate of yours so you can navigate. Back in a minute, Rick." With that, Bert and Paul started down the hall.

Rick walked over to the ash tray and crushed the smoldering cigarette. No one around his home had ever smoked, and even though he had tried it a couple of times, he had never started, so he was keenly aware of the smoke in the room. "So this is what I'm in for," he muttered to himself.

Since Rick had arrived first, he had selected his side of the room, and was busy putting his clothes in the drawers when the others returned. Paul was carrying two suitcases, and Bert had some stereo equipment under one arm, and a box of tapes under the other.

"Hope you don't mind a little music," Bert said. "I just brought a few of my tapes to keep us company."

"A few?" Paul chided. "You should see them. He's got more tapes than a disc jockey."

When Bert had finished unloading the car, his first move was to set up the stereo on the shelf under the window and select a cassette from the box and insert it in the tape deck. Then to the beat of a rock band, he began to unpack. When Rick finished putting away his clothes, he sat down on his bed and watched Bert.

"Who's the dame?" Bert asked, pointing a finger at the picture on Rick's desk.

"That's Ann. A girl back home," Rick answered. "She couldn't come this year—still a senior, you know."

"And I suppose you gave her all that jazz about being true?"

"Yes, as a matter of fact, I did. Why?"

"I did the same thing last year. Wow, did she ever get sentimental the last night! Cried all over my sweater. And you know what?" Bert turned around and pointed a clothes hanger at Rick. "I found out later that she was out with another fellow the very next night. She didn't mean a word of it. Come to think of it, neither did I."

"But it's different with Ann and me. We meant it . . . I think."

"That's what you think," Bert responded. "With five thousand women on this campus, and every one of them out to get a man, you'll change your mind in a hurry."

"We'll see," Rick said, shrugging his shoulders.

Bert stopped unpacking, leaned against the closet door, and pulled out a cigarette. "Look, Rick, I waited 18 years for this freedom. All my life I was told what to do, where to go, when to study, when to get in at night, and when to go to bed. Now I'm free! For the first time in my life I can stay up all night if I want to, with nobody nagging at me. And this freedom goes for women too. Back home there were only so many girls to go around, and you sorta had to stick with one to be sure you had a date, but that's not true here. The sooner you realize that you're away from home, and that the only thing that really matters is what you think, and what you want to do, the better you will enjoy this college bit."

Bert took a long draw on his cigarette, and then continued. "I'm not the first one to feel this way. My dad went to this college, and I'll bet if he ever got honest with me, he would admit he made the same decision when he came here. I've heard from some of his old college buddies he was quite a rounder. You stay true to your little woman if you want to, but as for me, I'm living for Bert—only Bert."

The room was silent now, and Rick sat staring at

the floor. Bert, apparently satisfied with his little speech, dropped into his chair and blew several well-formed smoke rings. It was Bert who finally broke the silence. "Man, this is living—really living!"

But there was little time for "living" during the remainder of the week. The schedule was filled with orientation meetings, counseling with advisors, registration, and, for Rick, Freshman entrance exams. It was Friday afternoon before Rick and Bert found themselves in the room again at the same time with some time to talk.

"What a rat race!" Bert exclaimed. "What did you get stuck with?"

"Intro to Psych, English, Math and Speech. How about you?"

"Sophomore English, Biology, Intro to Art, and Phys Ed. I tried to get into Psych, but it was closed by the time I went through the line. Somebody suggested Sociology. Wonder what its like?"

"How should I know," Rick laughed. "I can't even spell it."

"Come on, Rick, let's get out of this hole. There must be something going on in this town."

"I should write to Ann. Haven't had time all week."

"Let her wait another day. That way she'll think you are really having a tough time in college."

"You convinced me. Let's go. I can write to her tomorrow."

Rick picked up his car keys from the desk, and took a sweater from the closet. It was a high school letter sweater which had a large "B" in gold on a blue background.

"What's the "B" stand for?" Bert asked. "Baby?"

"Would you believe, best, bashful, beautiful . . ."

"And bewildered?" Bert cut in.

"Bewildered, yes," Rick said, laughing. "Come on, let's go."

2

Friday Night in Mill City

Mill City does not come as a surprise. As you drive through the flat, rich farmland of southern Minnesota, and suddenly drop into a stream-dissected valley, you expect a town to be there. All of the ingredients for the making of a town are to be found in the valley: a river, protecting bluffs, and a flat floodplain for a business district.

Mill City began in the early 1800s when settlers first moved into southern Minnesota. Boats came up the river from Minneapolis and St. Paul bringing supplies for the settlers, and exchanging them for wheat and salt pork. Because it is ideally located in a rich agricultural area, Mill City has continued to grow until now the sign at the edge of town reads, "POPULATION 26,532." Everyone knows it is more than that, especially when the students are in town, but no one has bothered to change the sign since the last census.

The one main street, appropriately named "Front" follows the river. A few more secondary streets run parallel to it on terraces which climb the bluffs like giant stair steps. The streets which dissect these at right angles, end abruptly against the sides of the valley, except for a few which wind through ravines and continue on to the upper level.

This arrangement makes possible a sort of natural segregation. Most of the workers live at the lower elevation in small frame two-bedroom homes with small yards filled with children and dogs. Some older, very large homes, which date from an earlier era, are still found in the valley, but they have been made into apartments for students who want more freedom than a dorm can give them.

And above all of this, looking down upon the valley from the edge of the bluffs, are large, newly-built homes occupied by wealthy merchants, equally wealthy retired farmers, and a few of the better paid college professors. When you look up at the bluffs from down-town, you have the feeling these homes are lifting their noses in haughty disdain to those who must stay in the valley.

So there are really three classes of people in Mill City—the wealthy, the workers, and the students. Each dislikes the other, yet each needs the other to survive.

The State College was organized in the latter part of the 19th century as a Normal Training School to supply teachers for that part of the state. It was originally built on one of the terraces overlooking the business district. But as enrollment grew and the school developed into a college, the older buildings were abandoned, and a new campus was built on some flat farmland about a mile from the center of town. It is just far enough away that most of the students use their cars for a trip into town.

Students who get tired of the confinement of the campus are limited as to where they can go and what they can do. Most of the time they simply drive from one end of Front street to the other. In the Fall and Spring, this is done with windows open and radios blaring, giving the downtown a carnival atmosphere.

Two or three places have become time-honored hangouts for the students. One of these is the *Ratskeller*, a three-two beer joint that makes an effort to check I.D. cards to be sure students are old enough to drink. It has live entertainment on the weekends, which usually consists of a combo made up of college students who get a few dollars and all the beer they can drink for their efforts.

Another favorite place, *The Kitchen*, is located at the north end of Front street, almost in the country. It is the place for those who aren't old enough for the *Ratskeller*, or who are not interested in drinking. It serves hamburgers, soup, and soft drinks, and lets students stay as long as they like as long as they occasionally buy something.

The students, their cars, and the noise, are constant sources of frustration for the local police and residents. The city appreciates the money which the college brings into the community, but it has never learned to appreciate the students who go with it. They are always looked upon with suspicion, and, at best, a necessary evil.

A favorite story, which every new group of students hears when arriving in town, involves a local cop who enjoyed parking his patrol car just out of sight at a downtown intersection. He would wait for some student to go by a little over the speed limit, and then he would take off after the student with lights flashing, and siren blaring.

The officer's parking spot was next to a popcorn stand built on wheels. It had been operated by the same old man for as long as anyone could remember. One evening, some students tied the popcorn stand to the back of the patrol car, and then proceeded to race down Front street. As expected, the officer gave chase only to find he was pulling a popcorn stand and a badly frightened old man behind him.

After Rick and Bert had driven up and down Front street several times, they decided to stop at *The Kitchen*. Most of the tables and booths were filled, but someone recognized Bert, and motioned for the fellows to join the group at his table. There were already three fellows and two girls at the table, but they pushed the chairs together to make room for two more.

"Hey, is this all there is to do in town tonight?" Bert asked when they were seated.

"Dullsville, isn't it?" one of the girls responded.

"You said it!" Bert replied.

"I heard there was a party going on somewhere," one of the fellows said.

"Where?" Bert asked.

"I suppose in the clearing south of town, that's

where they always are," another one answered.

"Well, what are we waiting for," Bert said, getting up from his chair. "Come on, let's go."

"Not me," the first fellow said. "I got my fill of it last year."

"Me, too," added the third fellow.

"Anything's better than just sitting here," one of the girls said.

"Yeah, we'll go with you," the other girl responded.

"Come along," Bert replied.

"Hey, wait a minute," Rick interrupted. "You forget it's my car."

"Aw, come on, Rick," Bert coaxed, pulling at Rick's sleeve, "you might just as well find out what life in this town is like."

Rick got up reluctantly, and followed Bert and the two girls out to the car. Bert opened the back door, and one of the girls got in with him. Rick went around to the driver's side, and by the time he was behind the wheel, the other girl was already in the seat beside him.

"So, where do we go?" Rick asked.

"Just go south on Front street. We'll tell you where to turn off," Bert replied.

Rick was beginning to wish he had stayed at the dorm, but there didn't seem to be any way to get out of the situation at the moment. Bert and the girl in the back seat began talking, but Rick remained silent.

"So, what's your name, O Silent One," the girl beside him asked.

"Rick Erickson," he answered, without taking his eyes off the road.

"Freshman?"

"Yeah, how could you tell?"

"It's easy."

"And you?" Rick asked.

"Sophomore."

"So, you've done this before?"

"Sure, lots of times," she answered.

"What goes on at one of these parties?" Rick asked.

"Wow, you *are* new, aren't you?" she replied.

"You didn't answer my question."

"Anything you want, I guess," she answered.

Rick didn't like the way she said, "anything," and his face obviously showed it.

"O, don't worry," she said. "You're a big boy now. You're in college, not kindergarten."

They went south on Front street through town, and then, following Bert's directions, Rick turned off on a little side road that ran along the river. After about a quarter of a mile, it became a one-lane trail, and a little farther on, it was blocked by a car.

"Here's where we get out," Bert said.

Rick shut off the motor, turned off the lights, and everyone got out of the car. As they started to walk, Rick could hear the sound of voices, and after a couple hundred feet more, he could see a clearing with some kids sitting around a fire.

When they arrived at the clearing, he found about twenty-five kids. Some of them were just sitting, smoking, and staring into the fire. Others were lying on blankets, and still others were walking around with a can of beer in their hands. Except for the cigarettes and the beer, it reminded Rick of the nightly camp fires he had witnessed all summer.

The girl who had come with Rick was still by his side, talking constantly, but Rick wasn't listening.

"How about a beer?" she asked, tugging at his arm.

Rick pulled his arm away and stammered, "No... no, thank you. I don..."

"I know. You don't drink. I've heard that before. What you mean is that you didn't drink at home. You're in a different world now. Everybody drinks here."

"Not quite everybody," Rick said firmly.

"Well, you don't have to get sore about it," she said. "Mind if I have one?"

"Why should I mind?" Rick said, walking away from her.

"Now don't go away, I'll be right back," she said as she moved toward the edge of the circle where a tub had been placed, filled with ice and beer.

Rick thought about leaving, but then remembered Bert. In the flickering light of the fire, he could see Bert sitting with a beer in hand, and totally engrossed in conversation with the girl who had come with him.

Rick went over and slapped Bert on the back. "Wow, you sure work fast," he said, laughing.

"Looks like you are getting hooked too," Bert replied.

"Look, Bert, I don't know if I want to stay."

"What? We just got here. Aw, come on, Rick, have a beer and enjoy yourself. Nobody's going to tell the little gal back home. Besides, that one looks like a pro, and you could learn a few things from her."

"That's what I'm afraid of," Rick said. This time he wasn't laughing.

"Oh, there you are," the girl said, coming out of the shadows. "I thought I told you to wait."

"I . . . aw . . . ," Rick stuttered.

"The name is Kandi."

"Oh, yes, Kandi. I'm in no mood for this kind of stuff. I had a long hard week, and I need to get back to the dorm."

"You poor overworked boy," she purred. "At least you can sit down and talk to me while I finish this beer."

Having run out of arguments, Rick followed Kandi to a spot in the shadows, and sat down beside her.

"Tell me," Kandi said, "why don't you drink? Is it because of some religious kick?"

"Well, I guess if you want to put it that way, yes. I am a Christian, and the crowd I ran around with all my life just didn't drink."

"You mean you've never been drunk?" Kandi said in a surprised voice.

"Not only that, I've only tasted the stuff a couple of times in my life."

"Wow, I didn't know there were such innocent birds left any more," she said, taking another swallow from her can.

"And the next thing you're going to tell me is that you don't smoke either," she said.

"That's right."

"Grass?"

"Never."

"Well, I have to admire your stand, but your life does sound rather dull to me," Kandi said, shaking her head.

When she finished her beer, she moved a little closer to Rick, and he could feel the warmth of her body. His mind began to wander to other nights—similar, but so very different. He remembered nights when Ann was sitting near to him like this, but instead of a beer it was a Coke, and instead of small talk, there were testimonies.

Kandi continued a steady stream of chatter. She talked about school, men, roommates, and life in general. Rick pretended to be listening by answering an occasional question, but his mind was several hundred miles away.

He was beginning to feel more comfortable now, and so he dropped back on the grass where he could look up at the stars. To his surprise, Kandi immediately followed, and put her head in the curve of his arm. As if by reflex, his arm tightened around her slender neck. It felt good to have a girl in his arms again. He realized how much he really missed Ann.

He and Ann had often been like this for hours, perfectly content just to feel each other near. But Rick soon discovered this wasn't Ann, and it was evident from Kandi's actions that she was expecting this to develop into something more. When he realized what was happening, he bolted upright, almost dumping Kandi to the ground.

"Why, of all the . . . ," she sputtered.

"Sorry, I didn't mean to hurt you," Rick said, getting up.

"And where do you think you are going?" she asked.

"Never mind," he answered, walking away.

Rick found Bert in the crowd and said, "Look Bert, I'm going. Here are the keys. You bring the car when you come."

And with that, he began to run.

The Morning After

When Rick awakened, he had the uncomfortable feeling that one often has after a nightmare. He buried his head under the pillow and tried to go back to sleep.

But the feeling persisted, and gradually it all began to come back...last night...the party...and Kandi. He could still hear her voice, "You'll never know until you try."

By now he realized it wasn't a dream, and he sat up in bed. From that position, he could see himself in the mirror. What a mess! His hair was tangled, he needed a shave, and his clothes were dirty and wrinkled. He hadn't bothered to undress when he got home—just pulled off his boots and dropped into bed. He looked down at his muddy boots and remembered the walk to the main road, and of catching a ride into town.

He glanced over at the other bed to see if Bert was

awake. It was empty, and the covers were still in place. Obviously, Bert had not been in all night.

It was then Rick remembered that he had given Bert the keys to his car. He jumped up and went to the window to see if he could see it in the parking lot. He scanned each row of cars, but there was no two-tone green '76 Plymouth to be seen. There were other '76 Plymouths, but none with that special combination of greens. It had needed a paint job when he bought it, so he had picked out his own colors.

Thoughts began to race through his mind. What if Bert had been in an accident? What if Bert had been hurt in his car? He could think of a thousand "what if's," so he had to find the car.

First, he needed to clean up. He grabbed a towel, threw it over his shoulder and started for the shower room. Everything was quiet on Saturday morning, even the lavatory. He dashed some water on his face. He didn't have time for a shower or shave now, he had to find Bert—and his car.

But where could he start to look? What could he do? By the time he hung up his towel, put on some clean jeans, and a pair of shoes, he had decided on a course of action. He would start by asking some of Bert's friends. He remembered that Paul had been at the party, so he started down the hall toward Paul's room.

Rick knocked a couple of times, and finally a sleepy voice from within said, "Come on in, the door's open."

Rick walked in and saw a mass of black hair protruding from beneath the covers.

"What do you want at this hour?" Paul mumbled.

"Sorry to wake you up," Rick said, "but do you know where Bert is?"

"How would I know where Bert is?" Paul replied, sounding annoyed.

"Just thought you might. He didn't come in last night, and . . ."

"Oh, last night . . . now I remember," Paul said, slowly sitting up and rubbing his eyes. "The last time I saw Bert he was running."

"Running?"

"Yeah. He was running 'cause the cops had come to break up the party."

"Cops?" Rick's mouth dropped open.

"Seems that someone tipped off the cops that there were some minors out drinking beer, and that's a no-no in this town."

"But what about Bert? Did he get away?"

"Don't know," Paul said. "I was too busy taking care of myself."

"Thanks loads," Rick said. "You really make a fellow feel good."

"Say, why are you so concerned about Bert?" Paul asked.

"I'm not concerned about Bert," Rick answered. "I'm concerned about my car. I left it with him last night."

"Now, that's different. I guess you do have something to worry about. You'll learn never to leave your car with Bert. He's been in more accidents than most of us have had dates."

"Again, I say, thanks for your help," Rick said sarcastically as he turned to leave.

"Hey, wait a minute," Paul said. "You might try that girl's apartment. Let's see, what was her name? Bert was with her when he left. It was Marcia somebody, and she was with a girl named Kandi."

Then Rick remembered. The girl who had latched onto Bert had been with Kandi Hawkins, and Kandi had said they were roommates. Maybe her name was in the school directory.

Rick left Paul's room and went back to his own. He dug out the directory and began to search. Sure enough, there was a Kandi Hawkins, and the address was listed as 405 South 5th, Apartment 5. Rick jotted down the address, stuffed it in his pocket, and started toward the door.

As he walked down the hall, he thought again about last night. After running away from Kandi, he wondered what she would say this morning. He wasn't looking forward to the meeting, but he had to find Bert—and his car.

Rick began walking toward town. There were few cars on the road on Saturday morning, so his chances of getting a ride were nil. But it was just as well, as the walk gave him more time to think. He was worried about his car, but he was equally concerned about facing Kandi again. He stopped once, and considered turning back, but then regained his courage, and continued on toward town.

Rick was able to locate 405 South 5th Street with little trouble. It was one of the older Victorian homes which had been made over into apartments. He walked through the massive wooden doors into the front hall. The ornate ceiling, and hand-carved banisters were reminders of a former grand era. Now, however, the doorways to what had once been a parlor and the dining room were covered with wallboard, and marked with apartment numbers. The floors and walls were badly in need of repair, and instead of light fixtures in the hall, there was just a cord hanging with one bare light bulb at the end.

Rick went up the stairs, and worked his way along a dimly lighted hall until he found apartment 5. He took a deep breath and knocked on the door. He waited, and when he heard nothing, knocked again. He was almost ready to leave when he heard some stirring, and someone coming to the door.

The door opened a crack—as far as the night chain would allow—and through the opening Rick could see Kandi's face. When he had left the party, he never dreamed he would see her face again at 9 o'clock the next morning.

"Well, of all people...it's the runaway!" Kandi said in a sleepy, but sarcastic voice. "What do you want?"

"Is Bert in there?" Rick asked, ignoring the sarcasm.

"How should I know," she replied cooly.

"You must know if there is a man in there," Rick replied.

"There's some man in the bedroom with Marcia, if that's what you want to know."

"In the bedroom?"

"Yeah. Marcia dragged someone home last night."

"I need to know if it's Bert," Rick insisted.

"Guess you can come in and find out," Kandi said, unhooking the chain. "You're obviously harmless." Again her words were sarcastic and cutting.

Rick entered a room that was littered with books, records, and clothes. Along one wall was an unmade sofa bed which Kandi had apparently been using.

"They're in there," Kandi said, pointing to the bedroom door.

"Can't you find out for me?" Rick asked.

"I never interfere with my roommate's activities. If you want somebody in there, you'll have to go get him."

Just then the bedroom door opened and Bert stepped out, dressed only in his Jockey shorts.

"What's all the noise?" Bert asked.

"Boy, am I glad to see you!" Rick said.

"That's not exactly what I thought you would say," Bert replied.

"Where's my car?" Rick asked. "You can stay out all night if you want to, that's your business, but not with my car."

"Calm down," Bert said. "I didn't hurt your car. There may not be much gas left in it, but I didn't hurt it. I'll get the keys."

Bert disappeared for a moment, and then came back. "There you go," he said, tossing the keys to Rick. "It's parked in the rear. Now, just go away and be quiet." With that he went back into the room and closed the door.

As Rick turned to leave, he found Kandi standing in front of the door with her arms folded.

"And where do you think you're going?" she asked.

"To the dorm where I belong," Rick snapped back.

"No, you're not," she said with a cross between a smile and a smirk on her face.

"And why not?"

"Because, you came here, got me out of bed on Saturday morning, and now the least you can do is stay and talk to me. I'm not going to let you run away like you did last night."

Kandi took Rick by the arm and led him to a soft chair. "You just sit here like a good boy while I make us some coffee," she purred, patting his arm.

Rick sat down like an obedient child and watched as Kandi crossed the room toward the kitchen area.

The entire apartment consisted of one large room which had, no doubt, been a bedroom in the old mansion. It served as both a living and an eating area. The kitchen was made in what had been the closet, and was only large enough for one to work in it at a time. Off this large room was a smaller room, now used as a bedroom, and a bathroom.

From Rick's chair, he could watch Kandi working in the kitchen. She rinsed out the coffee pot, put fresh water in it, and then inserted the basket. This was really his first opportunity to look closely at her. It had been dark the previous night, and she had been wearing jeans and an oversize sweatshirt. Now, he had a much better view. He could see the smooth, graceful curves of her body beneath the sheer negligee as she stretched to get something from a high shelf. The sun, shining through the tiny kitchen window, highlighted her shoulder-length blond hair. Her complexion, even without makeup, was flawless. Watching her made the problems of the morning begin to seem less important. He had all but forgotten that he had been forced to stay.

When the coffee pot was plugged in, she turned a large, well-worn, overstuffed chair around so that she could face Rick, then pulled her feet up under her and nestled back into the chair like a house cat preparing for an afternoon nap.

"O.K., tell me something about yourself," she began.

"Like what?" Rick asked.

"I just want to know what makes you tick. You seem so different, so mysterious behind those blue eyes."

"What you are really asking is why I didn't drink last night, and why I didn't come home and go to bed with you like Bert did with Marcia. Right?"

"That's kinda blunt, but I guess that's what I mean. Although I can't remember inviting you home."

"Sorry. I didn't mean to be quite that blunt, but for someone who has spent all of his life in a very different environment, this whole thing is quite a shock."

"Tell me about your crowd. They sound terribly dull."

Rick's mind went back to his last night at home. There had been laughter and fun, and it never occurred to him to think of the party as dull. But how could he explain this to Kandi. Her world was entirely different.

"I'm not sure you would understand," Rick began. "You see, my world has largely revolved around church and friends from church."

"I might have known . . . religion strikes again!" Kandi interrupted.

"What do you mean by that?"

"I mean that every time I've tried to have a good time, somebody . . . my parents, a friend, somebody, has thrown religion in my face. I came to school to get away from it, and here we go again!"

"I told you that you wouldn't understand," Rick insisted, and started to get up.

"Sit down," Kandi said sharply. The tone of her voice startled Rick, and made him drop back into the chair.

"If you really believe what you're saying, you can at least try to explain it to me," she said. "If you can't explain it, you had better forget it."

Rick had never been faced with this kind of challenge to his faith before. He often had to explain to the High School gang why he would not go to certain places, but he could usually get around that by pointing out certain church activities to which he had to go.

"O.K., you asked for it," Rick said, drawing a deep breath. "Like I say, I grew up in church, but that's not the basic reason for my actions, or lack of them. When I was twelve, I accepted Christ as my personal Savior."

"You what?"

"Let me finish," he said. Now that he had started, he didn't want to be interrupted. It was as if someone else was speaking, and he wanted to listen to what he had to say.

"Since that time," he continued, "I've spent a lot of

time thinking about life, and I've become convinced that I was placed here on earth for a purpose. Haven't you ever wondered why you're here?"

Kandi's eyes became serious. "Sure, doesn't everyone? At some time or other we all ask, 'Who am I?' or 'Why am I here?' "

"But I think I've found the answer," Rick said.

"And if you haven't, you're wasting a lot of valuable time by trying to be good and do what you think is right."

"But the answer is in the Bible, and I believe the Bible is true. It says that I can find purpose for living through faith in Jesus Christ."

Rick was gaining more confidence now, and so he continued. "If we were inanimate objects like parts of a car, it would be simple to discover our identity and purpose. We would simply wait for the mechanic-creator to place us in the right place in his machine. But we aren't machines. We are human beings, or at least we were intended to be. And human beings have wills, likes, dislikes, loves, hates, and we need to turn all of these things over to someone who can put them into some master plan. I believe that God has a plan for the universe, and that He can use me in that plan."

"But what does all that have to do with things like drinking and sex?"

"Well, if I have decided to give myself completely to God for His use, then I have to be careful and guard against any misuse. I must avoid anything which might prevent Him from getting the very best from me."

Rick was just beginning to feel comfortable when

his conversation was interrupted by Bert, now fully clothed, coming out of the bedroom.

"Did I smell coffee?" Bert said, sniffing the air.

"Why did you have to come out now?" Kandi said. "We were just getting serious."

"I heard, and I thought you should be rescued from that sermon," Bert replied.

Marcia was dressed now, and joined the group in the living room. The girls made breakfast while the fellows listened to some records. Then they all sat around a card table and ate bacon, eggs, and toast.

When they had finished eating, Rick got up to go and Bert followed. "I'd better go if I don't want to walk home," Bert said.

"Thanks for breakfast," Rick said. "Sorry that I spoiled your morning."

"You didn't spoil it," Kandi replied. "I rather enjoyed it. We've got to finish that conversation when we can be alone."

"I'd like that," Rick answered.

"Say, we're having some people over for a party next Saturday night. How about you fellows coming?" Marcia asked.

"Sure," Bert answered quickly, "we'll be here."

"Well, I'm not so sure . . . " Rick hesitated.

"Do come," Kandi said, and Rick could tell she was serious. "Maybe we can introduce you to another world. Who knows, you might like it."

"I'll think about it," Rick said as he opened the door.

Emancipation

Since classes hadn't started, there were no assignments to do, so Rick spent the remainder of Saturday doing various odd jobs. He washed his car at a coin-operated car wash, finished organizing his dresser drawers, and then spent the evening writing a long letter to Ann. Bert was gone when he got home from the car wash, and he was still gone when Rick decided to go to bed.

Although his body felt tired, his mind refused to go to sleep. He lay staring up at the dark ceiling, thinking back over the previous twenty-four hours. He was having difficulty sorting out his feelings. On the one hand, he felt guilty about having been at the beer party. He knew that he had done nothing wrong, but just being in the presence of activities which he considered wrong, gave him a feeling of "guilt by association."

On the other hand, he had a feeling of satisfaction

over the answers which he had given to Kandi. It was the first time he could remember ever really witnessing to someone who was a non-Christian. He had given testimonies many times before, but always to other Christians, usually at church or at camp. This time he had really witnessed, and it was a new, exhilarating experience.

When Rick awakened the next morning, the sun had already come up over the top of the dorms across the courtyard, and its warm rays were falling directly on his bed. He reached over to his desk and got his wristwatch. By closing one eye, he could get the other focused enough to see that it was already 10:30.

Rick remembered this was Sunday, and once again he had mixed feelings. The last time he had been in bed on Sunday morning at 10:30 he had the chicken pox, and was running a 101 fever. By this time any other Sunday morning his mother would have called, "Rick, get up, it's time to go to Sunday School."

But this morning there was no mother to awaken him. He had overslept, and he felt guilty about it. But since it was too late to go to church, he turned over in bed, and buried his head under the covers. Now, curled up in a warm bed, he somehow didn't feel quite so guilty. For the first time in his life he could stay home if he wanted to, and he had to admit to himself that he wanted to. A warm, satisfied feeling soon replaced the feeling of guilt, and he went back to sleep.

Eventually, others began to stir in the dorm, so Rick sat up in bed. He looked over at Bert's bed, and saw that he was awake too.

"When did you get in?" Rick asked.

"Don't know, and really don't care," Bert replied with a yawn. "Didn't you hear me?"

"Naw, it took me a long time to go to sleep, but once I made it, I was really out," Rick replied.

"I'm hungry," Bert said. "Let's get some chow."

"Sounds great," Rick answered, throwing back the covers.

The two got up, showered and shaved, then went down to the cafeteria for dinner. Bert's buddy, Paul, joined them at a table, and when they finished eating, Bert and Paul went off together, and Rick went back to his room.

First, he began to look through the pile of textbooks which he had purchased. He tried reading the first chapter in his Psych book, but found his mind kept wandering. Then he thumbed through the Speech book, and finally, for want of something better to do, he lay back down on the bed.

It was already beginning to get dark when he awakened. He got up and sat down at his desk. From there he could look out across the parking lot where the last rays of the sun were touching the tops of the cars and casting long shadows across the asphalt. Being alone like this was a new experience for Rick. He had always been active, always with a crowd, and now he was alone and 200 miles from home.

Rick glanced at his watch. It was now 6 o'clock. He remembered that the kids at church were now beginning to assemble for their weekly youth meeting. He could visualize each one. He wondered where Ann was sitting, and with whom. He could almost hear someone praying, "Lord, bless the kids who are away at college. Keep them, Lord, and protect them."

He had prayed that prayer a hundred times or more, but he never realized before just how much those college kids needed prayer. Before this, it had just been a routine prayer to him.

Rick put his head down on his arms and tried to pray. He prayed for the kids back at the church, and then began to pray for himself. "Lord, You know all about me. You know how much I need Your help. Please, Lord, help me to be a good witness for You."

A loud banging on the door brought Rick back to reality. It was totally dark now, and he stumbled against a chair on his way to the door. He flipped on the light and unlocked the door.

"Wow, you believe in seclusion," a fellow said.

"I was just . . . just taking a nap," Rick answered.

"It shows," the other responded.

Rick glanced at himself in the mirror, then laughed as he tried to straighten out his tangled hair. "Guess it does," he agreed.

"Say, I'm Wayne Larson, from down the hall. We're having a Bible study in my room tonight. How about joining us?"

"Who's us?" Rick asked.

"About five guys from this floor. We started it last year, and it grew to about ten, but some of the fellows graduated, so I don't know how many we'll have tonight. We try to keep it to about an hour, just in case somebody has to study. How about it?"

"Sure," Rick agreed. "Guess I don't have anything more important to do."

"Great. See you about eight." With that Wayne left.

Rick had just found his Bible which had never been unpacked, and was starting toward the door when Bert came in.

"Well, look at the preacher," Bert said.

"Aw, knock it off," Rick snapped, obviously annoyed.

"Now don't get sore—only kidding. Just that I never saw you . . . or anybody else carrying a Bible before. Where are you going?"

"If I'm needed, I'll be down in room 211—Wayne Larson's room."

"And if I'm needed, I'll be at Marcia's studying. Why don't you come with me? Kandi would love it, you know."

"Not tonight."

"What's the matter? Afraid?"

Rick blushed, opened his mouth to answer, but instead just turned and went out the door.

When Rick arrived at Wayne's room, the others were already assembled, so Wayne introduced him around. There was David Barr from a farm in Southern Minnesota. As he shook hands, Rick could feel the callouses which Dave had developed from working on the farm all summer. Then there was Tony Karas, a six-foot-five, two hundred and fifty pounder who Rick guessed must be a football player. Almost his direct opposite sat next to him. His name was Tim Conners, a skinny kid who looked more like a high school freshman. Wayne introduced him as a preacher's kid from Chicago. And there was Randy, a well-built fellow about Rick's size with a smiling handsome face, dark brown eyes, and a mass of dark brown hair parted in the middle.

Wayne acted as the leader, but it was just a loosely organized study with time for lots of discussion. Someone had decided that they would study the book of Romans, so they concentrated on the first chapter.

Once the Bible study began, Rick felt right at home. Even though all of the others were upperclassmen, they seemed to accept him immediately. He took his turn at reading Scripture and participating in the discussion.

At the close of the study, Wayne asked each one to pray, remembering specifically one other fellow in the dorm. When it came Rick's turn, the only one he could think of was his roommate, so he said, "Lord, thank You for the opportunity You have given to each one of us to witness for You. I pray for Bert..." Rick paused as a picture of Bert with Marcia and Kandi flashed through his mind. He wondered if Kandi was alone. Then he continued to pray. "Lord, help me to be a witness to them." He was immediately conscious of his use of "them," but it was too late to change and impossible to explain, so he just abruptly ended his prayer with an "Amen."

It was late when Bert returned to the room, but Rick was still sitting up in bed reading. He had slept most of the day, so he wasn't exactly tired.

"So, did you enjoy your Bible study?" Bert asked as he began to undress.

"Sure," Rick answered without looking up from his book.

"You did not," Bert responded.

Rick dropped his book and looked up. "What makes you say that?"

"Because I think you're a phony. I'll bet you sat there wishing you had gone with me."

Rick turned away from Bert's intense stare.

"You did, didn't you? You did think about us, didn't you?" Bert insisted.

"What's the matter with you, Bert, have you been drinking?" Rick asked.

"I'm stone sober," Bert answered. "You didn't answer my question."

"Why would that make me a phony?" Rick asked.

"If you were sitting there, mouthing pious words, and all the time wishing you were in bed with Kandi, I say you are a phony."

"Hey, Bert, I never said I was perfect. I'm as human as you, but there are some things I can't do."

"Why, because you're not man enough?"

"No, because I just can't," Rick said, almost pleading.

"Have you ever tried it?" Bert asked.

"No."

"Then how do you know you can't?"

"You don't understand. When I say I can't, I mean my conscience won't let me."

"I'm sure glad I don't have a conscience," Bert said, jumping into bed and pulling up the covers. Then, half sitting up, he pointed to Rick. "You know, kid, being my roommate may be the best thing that ever happened to your little world."

"I hope it works the other way around," Rick responded.

"No way," Bert answered, pulling the covers up over his head.

5

The Party

The following week Rick went to all of his classes for the first time, and by Friday night he was already loaded down with several reading assignments and a five-minute speech to prepare for Monday morning. Except for some frustrations in finding buildings and rooms, he had gotten along fairly well. By the end of the week, he had decided that maybe college wasn't going to be so bad after all.

Rick didn't see Kandi during the week except once and then they were on opposite sides of the library, and she didn't see him. He was glad for that because he wasn't really sure what more he could say to her if he did meet her.

When Friday night came, Bert went out as usual, and Rick used the time to write a letter to Ann, and begin his reading assignments. He went to bed about midnight, and never did hear Bert come in, although he was in his bed the following morning.

With this kind of a roommate, Rick was glad that he was a sound sleeper.

On Saturday night, when Bert was getting ready to go out, Rick said, "Don't you ever stay home and study?"

"Like I said the first day, I'm here for a good time," Bert answered. "I have no intention of working when there is something more interesting to do. I'm my own boss now, and I'm going to make the most of it."

"O.K., guess it's your life," Rick said, shrugging his shoulders.

"Aren't you going to the party?" Bert asked.

"Wasn't planning to," Rick answered.

"Kandi invited you, you know."

"I know. She probably did it only to be polite. I'm afraid I would spoil your kind of party."

"You don't know what you're missing," Bert said. "You've led such a sheltered life that you can't make valid comparisons. If you try my life, and don't like it, then you can preach to me, but right now, you don't even know what it's all about." With that he left the room.

Bert's words hurt. Rick knew that he had lived a sheltered life, and his old nature was curious to see what it would be like to get drunk, to spend a night with a woman as Bert had done, and to get high on drugs. He had always heard how wrong all of these things were, but he had never experienced them for himself. Maybe he had led too sheltered a life. Maybe it was time for him to do a little experimenting. Just then Bert came back into the room.

"Thought you left," Rick said.

"I did," Bert answered," but I forgot my cigarettes."

"Say, Bert."

"Yeah."

"I've been thinking. Maybe I will go with you after all."

"So you decided to join the human race," Bert said, sitting down on his bed. "Get ready. I have Paul's car for the night, so I'll wait for you."

When Bert and Rick arrived at the apartment, the room was already crowded. Kandi answered their knock, and ushered them in. She seemed pleased that Rick had come, and made a point of introducing him to everyone in the room.

Rick soon discovered that most of the kids were from the apartments in the area, rather than the dorms, so they were either Juniors or Seniors. He recognized one fellow from his Psychology class, and wondered why he was taking Freshman Psych. All of the others were strangers to him.

But they weren't strangers long. Rick had always made friends quickly, and this night was no exception. It wasn't long before several girls were crowded around him, and he was enjoying every minute of it. Except for the cigarettes, the beer, and an occasional glass of wine, this party was starting out like many others which Rick had attended back home.

By midnight, however, the noise level had increased significantly as the drinking was beginning to have its effect. One fellow, who had been unusually quiet earlier in the evening, began to walk around with a stack of records on his head to prove how sober he was. Every time the pile fell off, everyone would roar with laughter. Kandi finally rescued the records and hid them in the closet so that they wouldn't get broken.

About two A.M., somebody decided to send out for a pizza, but by the time it arrived, Rick was about the only one who was still in the mood for it.

When the party showed no signs of stopping, and it was three A.M. Rick decided he had had enough, and wanted to go home. He looked around for Bert, but couldn't find him. Somebody remembered seeing Bert and Marcia leave, but couldn't remember when, nor where they were going. Rick decided to wait for Bert. Since Bert had the car, it was either wait or walk.

Although it had been occupied much of the evening, Rick noticed that the bedroom was vacant, so he went in, took off his shoes and stretched out on the bed. He closed his eyes, and listened to the conversations in the next room. Somehow, most of them seemed so unimportant. The voices would rise to a crescendo, and then suddenly drop off almost to a whisper as if some conductor was leading them. There was a lot of nonsensical talk, but now and then Rick could hear snatches of a serious philosophical discussion going on between an ardent supporter of T.M. and a follower of Janism. Rick didn't know anything about either one, and at three in the morning, he really didn't care.

Soon the voices began to fade into the background and Rick turned over and buried his head in his arms.

When he awakened, light was shining directly in his eyes. For a moment, he thought that someone had turned on a light, but then realized it was the sun shining through the window. He vaguely remembered that it was Sunday morning and he didn't have classes, so he turned over in bed to go back to sleep. When he did, however, his hand touched something warm and soft, and he awoke with a start.

There, lying next to him was Kandi. Instantly, it all came back to him. He remembered the party and the noise. He listened, but all was quiet now. Kandi had obviously crawled into bed beside him with her clothes on. His first impulse was to get away as soon as possible, but then he began to study the sleeping form beside him. He raised up on one elbow to get a better look. She was even more beautiful than he had remembered. Her long blond hair lay in little uncombed puddles on the pillow. The sun pouring over her face accentuated her flawless complextion and long eyelashes.

Rick had a tremendous urge to reach over and draw the sleeping form to himself. His hand reached out, but just before it touched Kandi, he drew it back. Almost reluctantly he sat up, dropped his feet to the floor, and stood up. He looked back to see if he had awakened her. Once more he had the urge to stay. This was no doubt what Kandi had wanted all along, and here was his chance. He could hear Bert's voice saying, "You don't know what you're missing. You've led such a sheltered life, that you can't make comparisons."

It was true. He had never been in this situation before, and had never had this opportunity before. What's more, he might never have it again.

So he took a step back toward the bed, but then in a sudden surge of conviction, he turned, picked up his shoes, and headed back toward the door. He carefully opened the door and stepped into the living room, closing the door behind him. He listened for a moment to see if he had awakened her. When he heard nothing, he surveyed the room before him. Beer cans, records, and papers were everywhere, and there on the sofa were Bert and Marcia. They were covered by a sheet, and their clothes were in two piles on the floor. The sight was repulsive to Rick, and he headed for the door.

He quietly took off the night latch, and stepped out into the hall. After he closed the door, he remembered that he had left his jacket inside, but he wasn't going back for it now.

The streets of Mill City were empty on Sunday morning with the exception of a few cars which had begun to arrive at a little white frame church. He was reminded that it was Sunday, so he decided that he should go to church this morning. He wasn't sure where, but he would go to church, but first he had to get cleaned up.

Rick started to walk in the direction of the campus. He had fully expected to walk the entire distance, but a maintenance man on his way to work stopped and gave him a lift.

Rick's steps echoed down empty halls as he went to his room. It was a strange, lonely sound. On any class day these halls would be filled with students on their way to class throwing insults at those who were still in bed.

Rick threw a towel over his shoulder and started

down the hall for the showers. When he entered the room, he heard one of the showers running. As he undressed and went toward an empty stall, he noticed the nude form of Wayne Larson under the running water.

"Hi. Kinda empty here," Rick shouted over the sound of the water.

Wayne shut off the faucet, and stepped out of the shower stall. "I guess there aren't too many interested in getting up on Sunday morning," he said, reaching for his towel.

"So, what are you doing up?" Rick asked.

"Me?" Wayne said. "I guess Sunday wouldn't be Sunday if I didn't go to church—so here I am, a creature of habit after twenty years. And you?"

"Same here. I thought I would try to find one. Know any good churches in town?"

"Sure, how about going with me?" Wayne said. "I've been attending an interdenominational Campus Church downtown. Good preacher. The girls are bad news, but the preacher is good. How about it?"

"Sure, why not? Meet you in half an hour," Rick answered.

"In my room?"

"Yeah. I'll come by for you. We can use my car."

"Funny how a shower and a shave can make the world look different," Rick thought as he finished combing his hair. He took one more look in the mirror. His conscience even felt better this morning— he was going to church.

Once Rick and Wayne sat down in church everything seemed so right again. Once more he was at home with himself. What a different world this was from last night's party! This was the world he had grown to know and love. The party, the crowd—even Kandi—seemed miles and years away.

They stood to sing, "Great is Thy Faithfulness." About halfway through the song, Rick stopped singing and began to smile. "What would Kandi think if she could see me this morning?" he wondered. He looked quite different in his grey slacks and sport coat from the boy in blue jeans and sweater who got out of her bed that morning.

The song was over, and he and Wayne sat down. It felt good to sit as he hadn't had too much sleep, and the early morning walk had made him tired. The choir was singing now, but it wasn't a familiar song to Rick, so once again his mind began to wander.

But then came the sermon, and Rick was totally captivated by the message. The pastor was a young man. "Good for a college town," Rick thought. He was wearing a robe, but his boyish face sticking out of the black velvet collar seemed out of place. "Must be his first church," Rick thought.

The pastor read his text from Matthew 5:16. "Let your light so shine before men, that they may see your good works, and glorify your Father which is in heaven."

He talked about a dark world, and the need for more light. Then he looked at his young audience and said, "The only light this world can see, the only light this town can know, the only light your school can experience, is the light which shines through you. Let your light shine. It is a supernatural light, yet you can turn it on and off by your deeds and actions.

"Am I talking to someone here today through whom God could shine at one time, but now, either by sins of omission or commission you have turned off that light, and the world around you—your world—is dark because its only source of light has been extinguished?"

Rick began to think back over the previous two weeks, and wondered. Was his spiritual light already growing dim? He wondered what was really happening to him.

But then the service was over, and Rick and Wayne walked out of the church. They got into Rick's car and drove several blocks before either of them spoke. Finally Wayne said, "Great, wasn't it?"

"Huh? Oh, you mean the sermon? Yeah, it was great, but, as you said the girls were horrible."

Blue Monday

After dinner Rick went back to his room and tried to do some reading, but each time he began a paragraph, a picture of Kandi lying beside him would flash through his mind, and he would forget what he was reading.

Toward evening Bert came in. "Why didn't you wait for me this morning," he asked, throwing his sweater on the bed.

"You were asleep, and I wanted to go to church," Rick answered without looking up from his book.

"What's the matter, you needed to confess something?"

Rick turned and faced Bert. "What did I do that needs confessing?"

"Wow, you're changing even faster than I thought you would," Bert replied.

"What do you mean by that?"

"You should know. Kandi told me about it."

"What did she tell you?" Rick was standing up now and facing Bert.

"She told me what happened last night."

"Bert, nothing happened between Kandi and me."

"That's not what she said."

"You mean she told you that there was something between us. Why that little . . ."

"Watch it, Sunday School boys don't get mad either," Bert said, pushing Rick aside so that he could get to his dresser.

"I'm telling you that nothing happened," Rick insisted.

"That's your version," Bert said, throwing a towel around his neck.

"But that's the truth."

"Prove it," Bert called back over his shoulder as he went out of the door, leaving Rick standing in the middle of the room.

Rick stared at the closed door in disbelief, and then sat down on his bed. His mind swung wildly back and forth between sorrow and anger. He felt sorry for himself for getting blamed for something he didn't do, and he was angry with himself for listening to Bert and going to the party.

And he was angry with Kandi too. She was telling a lie, and she knew it. He felt his face getting flushed as he imagined the conversation which had gone on after he had left the apartment.

He was still in a bad mood when Wayne came by to see if he was going to Bible study.

"Sorry, Wayne, I just can't tonight," Rick said.

"Something the matter?" Wayne asked. "You look

like you just saw a ghost."

"I did," Rick said under his breath.

"You what?"

"Never mind. I just can't go anywhere tonight," Rick said emphatically.

"O.K., you don't have to if you don't want to," Wayne said, turning to leave. "But we'll miss you," he added as he went out of the door.

"Maybe next week," Rick called after him.

When Bert came back to the room, Rick pretended to be working at his desk, and neither spoke. Rick listened as Bert changed clothes, and left the room. As soon as the door was closed, Rick went back to bed.

It was after midnight when Bert returned. Rick was still awake, but he pretended to be asleep by burying his head under the pillow.

When the alarm went off on Monday morning, Rick had only been asleep for a couple of hours. To make matters even worse, his mind started right where it had left off the night before, and it made him feel as if he hadn't slept at all.

Rick's mood had changed little when he went to his first class. Freshman English wasn't too palatable to Rick at any hour, and at 9 o'clock on Monday morning, after a bad night it was downright miserable.

It was about halfway through a lecture on dangling participles that Rick asked himself, "What am I doing here?" At first it was just a flicker of an idea, but the longer he thought about it, the stronger the question came back to him. "What *am* I doing here?"

He thought about his parents, and the fact that they did not have a college degree. They had done O.K. in life. Why couldn't he just have stayed home, gone to trade school, and gotten a job? Where did he ever get the idea of needing a college education? He tried to think of a time when he had decided to go to college, but he couldn't. It seemed that he had just always considered it the thing to do.

He couldn't even remember praying about it. He just assumed that it was God's will for his life. But was it? Maybe the problems of the last forty-eight hours were indications that he was out of the will of God, and shouldn't be in college.

His daydreaming ended abruptly when the others around him began to close their books signaling the end of the hour. He looked down at his open notebook. At the top of the page he had carefully written, October 12, but the remainder of the page was blank except for a few doodles. As he left the classroom, he knew it would be useless to try to sit through another class. So, instead of going to Psychology, he crossed the mall, and entered the student union.

Rick poured himself a cup of coffee, and went through the cash register line. He normally didn't drink coffee, but he needed something stronger than milk this morning. He made his way to a table in a corner where he could be alone. He began to sip his coffee slowly, and let his eyes wander back and forth across the tables filled with laughing, noisy students.

Their laughter irritated him this morning. Why

should the whole world be so bright and happy when he was so unhappy? This was a new role for him. In high school he had always been in the middle of the crowd, and if there were laughter, he was probably helping produce it.

But Rick's solitude was short-lived. He was only halfway through his cup of coffee when someone pulled out the chair beside him and sat down. Rick turned, and recognized Randy Ellingson, one of the fellows from the Bible study group.

"Hi, Rick, mind if I join you?"

"Naw, have a seat," Rick said. He wasn't in the mood for company, but if he had to talk to someone, he was glad it was Randy. Of all the guys at the Bible study, he liked Randy best.

"Say, aren't you supposed to be in Psych?" Randy asked.

"Yeah, how did you know?"

"My roommate is in your class. When I got back to the room after our Bible study last night, I mentioned you, and he said that he knew you."

"Didn't know anybody knew me," Rick responded. "Who's your roommate?"

"Stu Miller."

"Never heard of him."

"He's a scared Freshman kid. He said you were the only one who spoke to him the first day, so he's been sitting beside you ever since."

"Oh, yeah, I remember him. He was so nervous the first day, he couldn't even sign the attendance card. But I can't remember doing anything special for him."

"You talked to him! In this big, impersonal university, all you need do is look interested in somebody, and they can't believe it. I told him you were a Christian, and that it was typical of Christians to pay attention to the individual."

"Gee, thanks for broadcasting it," Rick snapped.

"Sorry. Didn't know you would mind," Randy said, obviously taken back by Rick's reaction.

Rick looked up and saw the hurt expression on Randy's face. "Sorry, Randy. I'm in a bad mood this morning. It's O.K. Really it is."

They sat in silence a few minutes, and then Rick set his cup down and said, "Randy, why did you come to college?"

"Guess I thought it was the thing for me to do,"Randy answered.

"But, how did you know it was the thing for you to do?"

"I guess I would have to say that I felt led of the Lord to come here," he said.

"You mean that you are really sure that God led you to Southern State?"

"Yeah, guess so."

"But how did He lead you? How did you know?"

"Well, first, I did a lot of praying about it."

"What Christian doesn't? But I want to know how He answered. How did He tell you what to do?"

"I can't point to any one thing. I just became more and more convinced that this was the thing to do, and so I made plans accordingly."

"And you were sure they were right?"

"If you're where God wants you to be, it seems to me that you can just kinda go ahead and make plans, and He will let you know that everything is

O.K."

"I wish I could be that sure," Rick said thoughtfully.

"Don't give up yet, Rick. The first few weeks are always rough. It's a rude awakening to come out of a close-knit community and church and get dropped into the middle of this big pond, but you can't judge your whole college career by these first three weeks. Why don't you just go home and get some sleep. It will all look better tomorrow."

"Well, if it isn't the runaway!" Rick recognized the voice and was afraid to look up. Without waiting for an invitation, Kandi dropped her books on a chair, and sat down across from Rick and Randy.

Rick gave a quick look at Randy to see his expression. He wasn't really ready for these two to meet, but he was trapped.

"Randy, this is Kandi Hawkins. Kandi, this is Randy Ellingson."

Kandi tossed her long hair over one shoulder and smiled at Randy. "Hi, handsome."

"What's with this runaway bit?" Randy asked.

"Never mind," Rick snapped.

"Recognize this?" Kandi said, pulling something from beneath her pile of books.

"I should," Rick answered.

"You shouldn't leave jackets in girls' bedrooms," Kandi teased. "They can be used as incriminating evidence."

"I'm beginning to see what you meant by runaway," Randy said, "and I think it's time for me to go."

"Don't go now," Rick said almost pleading.

"I never interfere in domestic quarrels. It isn't

71

healthy." With that Randy picked up his books and walked away.

After Randy was a safe distance away, Kandi and Rick's eyes met. "O.K.," Rick said, "you've had your fun."

"What's the matter with you," Kandi said. "I just get you in hand, and when I turn around you're gone. That's twice you've done that."

"I told you that I have principles."

"I know, you said that before," Kandi answered. "But I've never met a man yet whose principles couldn't be compromised in some way."

"Now, Kandi, I didn't touch you Saturday night."

"I know."

"Then why did you tell Bert that I did?"

"Because I have principles. You don't think I was going to let Marcia get ahead of me, do you?"

"You mean you deliberately lied about it?"

"That's a hard word, but if that's what you want to call it, yes. I like to think of it as doing the necessary thing in the situation, and as I see it, that makes it right."

"But you lied! Didn't you consider what it would do to my reputation?"

"Your reputation? Don't you see that I was defending you. You wouldn't want Bert to think you were too immature or too chicken to go through with it when you had the opportunity, would you?"

"If that's what you call help, I don't need it. You just don't understand. You don't know my value system. You are so unprincipled that you can't tell right from wrong."

"Now you're preaching. That's what happens

when you go to church all your life. Anyway, let's not talk about it. Let's talk about Randy. Wow, what a hunk of humanity!"

"You leave him alone."

"What's the matter? You afraid that I might hurt him?"

"I just don't want him getting mixed up with someone like you. I'm sorry I ever met you."

"That makes me sound like a devil."

"Maybe you are," Rick answered. "Innocent men like me can only see that beautiful blond hair, and not the horns under it."

"Why, that's the nicest thing you've ever said," Kandi purred.

"Aw, come on, I'm hungry. Let's get something to eat."

7 Psych Class

Rick slept most of Monday afternoon. He got up long enough to eat dinner, and then went back to bed. By Tuesday morning, he was ready, both physically, and mentally, to face the world again.

Since he had missed Psych on Monday, he decided to go to class early, hoping to find someone who could tell him what had happened the day before. When he arrived at the room, he was surprised to find only three people—two fellows and a girl. The previous week there had been so many students that extra chairs had to be brought in.

He wondered if he was in the wrong room, so he stepped back into the hall to check the number on the door. It was the right number and the right building, so he walked back in. As he did, the other three, who were all sitting in the front row, turned around. One of the fellows, who Rick recognized as

Stu Miller, Randy Ellingson's roommate, waved his hand and called, "Come on down and join us."

Rick walked down the aisle and took a seat by Stu. "Where's everybody?" he asked.

"You obviously weren't here yesterday," the girl answered.

"No, I wasn't," Rick said, "and it's obvious that I missed something important. Want to clue me in?"

"This is a question and answer day," she answered.

"So, what is that?" Rick asked.

"Dr. Leonard is setting aside each Tuesday for questions and answers. Instead of a lecture, anyone who has a question can come to class and get it answered. The others can go to the library and read."

"And you have questions?"

"Sure, don't you?" she answered.

"Don't know," Rick responded. "You have to know something first before you know if you don't know."

"Hey, that sounds philosophical," Stu said, laughing.

Just then Dr. Leonard made his appearance. He looked more like a college student than a professor, but Rick had read his credentials in the college catalog, and knew that he must be older than he looked. He had received his doctorate at Stanford, and had taught at Southern for several years. Leonard was wearing blue jeans and a sweat shirt, so it was hard to distinguish him from the students.

Leonard seated himself on the desk, facing the four students, and pulled his sneakers under him so that he was sitting, cross-legged, like a guru before his disciples.

"So, I'm here, and you're here," he began. "Now where should we start?"

There was an awkward silence, then one of the fellows said, "I've been reading that chapter on stimulus and response, and it seems to me that most of the experiments have been done with rats, and yet most of the conclusions have been applied to humans. Does that make sense?"

"It is true that most of the classic experiments from Pavlov to Skinner have been made on dogs, chickens, pigeons, mice, rats, monkeys, etc., but since the nervous systems of most mammals have basic similarities, it is legitimate to make these comparisons."

"But it all seems to be so mechanistic," the first fellow said.

"What's wrong with that?" Dr. Leonard answered. "We live in a mechanistic world."

"But can't human beings make rational choices," Stu Miller asked.

"Most of your basic responses are the result of conditioning. Surely man is capable of making some rational, intelligent choices, but even the way he chooses is often the result of prior conditioning. Take for instance, you go to a party, and someone brings drugs. If you have been told often that drugs are bad, harmful, you will probably choose not to take any. But, you see, even that choice is the result of conditioning in which you have made an association between drugs and evil. On the other hand, if you have tried them and have found the experience to be pleasant, you will probably participate. You have been conditioned by a good response, just as Skinner's rats were conditioned."

"How about sex?" Rick asked.

"Yeah! How about it?" one of the other fellows exclaimed, and the others laughed.

"The sex drive is one of man's basic instincts, but even that can be conditioned through certain stimulus-response patterns."

"Like, man, who needs a stimulus?" one fellow said.

"I mean your sexual preferences and habits are the results of conditioning. You don't say to yourself, 'Now I'm going to be sexy.' If a nude model would walk across this platform, each of you fellows would react in a different way. Some of your reactions would be based upon your physical makeup, but most of them would be based upon your prior sexual education and experiences."

"What experiences?" Rick said, half under his breath.

"Experimentation is a normal maturing process," Dr. Leonard explained. "Society tends to put certain limits on that experimentation, but those limits are becoming fewer and fewer in our society."

"Isn't there a moral issue involved here?" Rick asked.

"Morals are nothing more than codes which individual societies have set up," Dr. Leonard answered.

"But aren't there some universal standards," the

girl asked.

"Maybe a few," Dr. Leonard answered. "But codes of sexual conduct vary greatly from culture to culture. What is sanctioned in one society is frowned upon by another."

"But, I mean, aren't there some things which are always right in all cultures and at all times?" the girl asked.

"For that to be true, you would need some ultimate, higher authority which would transcend all cultures," Dr. Leonard responded.

"There is such an authority," the girl said confidently. "God has set down certain rules for human conduct in the Bible."

"But isn't the Bible merely a reflection of the cultures in which it was written?" Dr. Leonard answered.

Rick couldn't keep quiet any longer. "It's true that the Bible was written in many different cultural contexts, but it still teaches the same standards throughout."

"That's not true," Dr. Leonard shot back. "What about polygamy in the Old Testament? What about having both a wife and a mistress as many did in the Old Testament? Are either of these sanctioned in the New?"

"Hey, let's get back to Psych," one of the fellows interrupted.

"Yes, maybe we had better do that," Dr. Leonard answered. "But, I'd like to discuss this more with you, aw . . . let's see . . . what's your name?"

"Rick."

"Yeah, Rick, let's talk about this later."

The remainder of the hour was spent discussing some technical questions about material in the text, and the subject of God did not come up again.

As the group started to leave at the end of the hour, Dr. Leonard said, "Rick, would you come here a minute?"

Rick approached the desk where the professor sat. "How about coming to my apartment some night and finishing our discussion?" Dr. Leonard said.

"Sure, why not?" Rick said, shrugging his shoulders.

"That's great," Leonard said. "What about next Wednesday—a week from tomorrow?"

"I'm free, as far as I know."

"Then come about 6 o'clock. We can have dinner together. I live just across the street from the campus. My address is in the school directory."

"O.K., I'll be there," Rick answered in a less-than-enthusiastic voice. The thought of defending his faith alone, and before a college professor, gave him some uneasiness, but he didn't know how he could get out of it now.

When he left the room, the girl from the class was waiting in the hall for him. "Wow! Thanks for helping me," she said as they began walking down the hall.

"That's O.K.," Rick said, blushing a little. "I couldn't let him say those things without saying something."

"Funny how hard it is to think of something to say at a time like that," the girl continued.

"Yeah, I know what you mean. I haven't had too much experience at defending what I believe. Most of the people I've been around either agreed with me or didn't care."

"You sound like you are a Christian," the girl said.

"Yes, I am. Does it show?" Rick replied.

"Sure, it shows. The way you answered Dr. Leonard, I could tell immediately."

They were outside now, walking from the Science building to the Student Union. The sidewalk was crowded with students hurrying to and from class, but Rick and the girl were oblivious to everyone around them. Rick's face was serious, and he was looking off in the distance as if in search of something.

"But it just didn't make sense," he said, as if talking to himself.

"What didn't?" the girl asked.

"The things I said."

"They did too. They are the same answers I've heard all my life."

"That's just the point," Rick said, stopping abruptly and pulling the girl around so that she faced him. "That's the point—everything I said in there I've heard a thousand times before, but does that make it right? Could it be that I was just mouthing something I've heard all my life? That really wasn't me talking in there. It was my pastor, camp counselors, parents, and ...," his voice trailed off.

The girl stared at him, frightened by the intensity of his voice. Finally, she looked away, and so did he, and they began walking again—this time in silence.

As they got to the steps of the Student Union, the girl said, "We really don't know ourselves very well, do we?"

"I thought I did," Rick answered, "but three weeks in this place has made me question everything—even myself."

"I've heard people talk about an identity crisis, but I never thought it would come this soon," the girl said.

"Kinda frightening, isn't it?" Rick said.

"Yeah, but exciting," the girl answered. "The questions always come before the answers."

"I'm afraid that some of us were taught the answers before we knew the questions," Rick answered.

"But does that make them wrong?" she said, turning away.

Rick watched her until she had turned the corner and was out of sight, and then he went into the Union for a cup of coffee.

A Crusade

When Rick got back to the dorm on Friday afternoon, he found a letter waiting for him. Even through the little window in his mailbox, he could tell it was from Ann—he had given her that stationery last year for her birthday.

As he walked up the two flights of steps to his room, he remembered how exciting he had imagined it would be to receive a letter from Ann. It had been exciting the first few times, but now everything was beginning to look different. Somehow home, church, high school, and even Ann seemed like a world away—a world that wasn't to mix well with his new world.

He stretched out on his bed and began to read. The letter was filled with news of familiar people and places. He could envision it all, but looking at it from the outside was much different than being a part of it. The after-game stop at the local hangout which

Ann described in great detail now seemed very juvenile to Rick. The chatter about who went with whom, and who had been selected as cheerleaders, and who had won the game, seemed totally meaningless in comparison to the questions with which he had been wrestling all week.

He was still holding Ann's letter when someone knocked.

"Come on in," Rick called. "Door's unlocked."

"Glad I found you home," Wayne Larson said, coming into the room.

"I'm here, but I'm not sure it's home," Rick said, laughing.

"Guess there is a difference." Then pointing to the letter in Rick's hand, Wayne asked, "Letter from the little woman?"

"Yeah, how can you tell?"

"Simple. Only a letter from a woman could put that glassy look in your eyes."

"I'm afraid it's more like a fog," Rick responded. Then changing the subject quickly, he said, "So what's on your mind?"

Wayne sat down on Bert's bed, and Rick sat up so that he was directly across from him. "We need your help, Rick."

"Who's we?"

"The guys in the Bible study. I'm sure there will be others, but right now it's just our group."

"So, what can I do?"

"Well, there is a bill before the state legislature to make drinking legal in the dorms. It's still illegal in this state, you know."

"What's that got to do with me?"

"We think that Christians should unite and try to do something about this. We need to show the world that there are some students who don't approve of drinking. According to the papers, every student at Southern spends his or her entire weekend drunk, and we want to tell the world that it isn't so."

"Again, I say, where do I fit into the picture?"

"Well, we were talking about it at Bible study Sunday night, and thought that you could represent the Freshman class at a rally we're having a week from next Monday. We'll invite the state representative from this area, and the local members of the board of regents, and we'll get some advertising in the local paper . . ."

"Whoa! Wait a minute," Rick said. "What do you mean by a class representative?"

"I mean that we will have a little speech from a member of each class . . ."

"Me, a speech?"

"Sure, you. You're articulate. You've got that self-assurance that it takes to make a public speech, and beside that, you look like a clean-cut all-American boy that any public official would listen to. You've got that kinda innocent look that would make your speech more believable. Some of the rest of us look like junkies, even if we aren't."

"Thanks for the compliment . . . I think," Rick said. "But being innocent isn't always an asset."

"I didn't say you were innocent," Wayne laughed. "I just said you *looked* innocent."

"I'll pretend I didn't hear that," Rick replied. "Now, tell me, where is this wake going to be held?"

"We've reserved the activities room here in the dorm. It should hold about 200, and I suspect that we might get more than that out if we advertise it right."

Rick was backed into a corner. It wasn't that he was afraid to get up before people. He had always volunteered to give speeches in High School, but this seemed different. This was for real—real people—real problems, and that made it different.

"You will do it, won't you?" Wayne asked.

Rick looked down at the floor for a few moments. Finally, not being able to think of a good reason to refuse, he said, "All right, I'll try it, but you'll have to tell me what to say."

"I'll even write the speech for you if you want me to," Wayne said jubilantly. "I can write, but I would faint dead away if I had to stand before that crowd."

He got up to go. "We'll talk about it on Sunday night. You'll be at Bible study won't you?"

"Yeah, I'll be there," Rick answered. "One of these weeks I should go home, but I guess it can wait."

"Good. See you Sunday."

Rick had never really been a crusader. This was partly due to the fact that there really wasn't anything to crusade about in his little world. One time people in his suburb got up-tight when Alex Krantz, a local drugstore owner, started selling adult magazines. The pastor asked everyone to go to the city council meeting and voice disapproval of this action. Rick had gone with a group of young people from the church, and carried a sign reading, "KEEP OUR DRUGSTORE FREE OF SMUT," but by the time the group got to the meeting, Krantz had heard of their protest, and had decided to pull the magazines off his shelf. Excepting for a minor skirmish like this, nothing really big had ever happened in his world which called for a crusade.

But Rick took his assignment seriously. He went with Wayne to church on Sunday morning, and then spent the afternoon in the library doing some background reading on the subject. By evening, when he went to Bible study, he was ready to make plans for the upcoming rally.

Rick found the same group in Wayne's room that had been there two weeks earlier. Several mentioned to Rick that they had missed him the previous week, but he offered no explanation for his absence.

The study was still in Romans 1. He found that they had become involved in a discussion the previous week on why Paul had said that the gospel was to the Jews first. This had taken up so much of the evening that they were only as far as verse 18.

Since the verses under discussion this night addressed themselves to perversion, that soon became the major topic of discussion.

"What should be our attitude toward someone who is gay?" Wayne asked.

"Don't know, never met one," Randy said.

"That's what you think," Tim Conners spoke up. "You meet them every day."

"Here at school?" David Barr said, looking shocked.

"School, town, everywhere. They're all over," Tim answered.

"How do you know?" Rick asked.

"Maybe kids from Chicago know more about life than we do," Randy said.

Everyone laughed except Tim. "Look fellows, it's no laughing matter. Statistics show that at least one out of every ten males have homosexual tendencies. They need our help."

"Glad there's only six of us here," Randy said.

Once again everyone laughed.

But Tim was obviously annoyed. "I thought we were supposed to be Christians," he said.

"We are, and we're saying that we're against the gay lifestyle," Randy said, getting serious.

"Can't we be against their lifestyle and still love them as individuals?" Tim asked.

"I can't see much love for them in these verses. In fact, God says that they will receive the due penalty of their error," Randy answered.

"I'm glad that God's my judge instead of you," Tim said.

"How can you tell if someone is gay?" Tony Koras asked.

"In most cases you can't," Tim answered. "Most of them are afraid to let anyone know. It could be one of your friends. It could be your roommate."

Rick laughed. "Not mine!"

"How do you know?" Tim asked.

" 'Cause he's too busy chasing girls to have time for fellows," Rick answered.

"Around the locker room there's talk that even some of the faculty members are queer," Tony Koras said.

"That's possible," Tim answered. "But why speculate on who is and who isn't. Why don't we discuss what the Bible says about it, and how we can help these fellows."

"Which sin is worse, fornication or homosexuality?" Rick asked.

"Sin is sin. They are both sins against the body and against the natural use of the body," Wayne answered. "The key verse for me is still I Corinthians 3:16." He found the verse in his Bible and read, "Do you not know that you are a temple of God and that the Spirit of God dwells in you? If any man destroys the temple of God, God will destroy him, for the temple of God is holy, and that is what you are."

The discussion continued for another half an hour, and in the end, it was decided that all of them would look up Scriptures on sexuality during the week, and bring them the following Sunday night for discussion. Wayne suggested that they should close the Bible study and spend some time planning the rally. So, as usual, they closed with prayer, first going around the circle asking for prayer requests.

"I wish you would pray for my roommate, Stu Miller," Randy said. "He came back from Psych class this week full of questions about God and the Bible. He said there had been a discussion about religion that had started him thinking. Pray that I may be able to lead him to Christ."

"I was involved in that discussion too," Rick said. "I contradicted Dr. Leonard a couple of times, and as a result, he has asked me to come to his house for dinner on Wednesday evening to discuss the matter further. Pray that God will give me the words to say, 'cause I can't match wits with that guy."

"Be careful of him," Tim said.

"What do you mean?" Rick asked.

"Just that. Be careful. He's got an answer for everything."

There wasn't time for Rick to pursue the subject as the next one gave his prayer request, but he wondered what Tim meant.

Following the prayer time, they spent the remainder of the evening talking about the next week's rally. By the time their group broke up, they had planned the entire affair, including who would take care of each detail, and what Rick should say in his speech.

It was almost midnight when Rick got back to his room, and to his surprise, Bert was home.

"Didn't expect to see you here," Rick said, putting his Bible on the desk.

"This is my room too, you know," Bert snapped, hanging his coat in the closet.

"Sorry. Just that you don't come around here too often before midnight."

Both of them proceeded to get ready for bed in silence. After they were both under the covers, and the lights were out, Bert said, "Didn't mean to snap at you. It's just that it was a bummer for a night. Things didn't go too well between Marcia and me."

"Sorry," Rick responded.

"I sorta envy you," Bert said.

"Envy me? Why?"

"You've got such self-control."

"What do you mean by that?" Rick asked.

"You don't have to go to bed with every female you meet, like me," Bert replied.

"But you said I did just last week."

"I know, but Kandi admitted to me tonight that she had made it all up."

"Sounds like you were talking about me again."

"That's all Kandi wanted to talk about," Bert said.

It was Rick's turn to be silent. He began to imagine the scene in Kandi and Marcia's apartment. He could hear Kandi's voice, see her smile, her golden hair, and her lovely figure, and soon he was wishing he could have been there. He finally went to sleep wondering just how much self-control he really did have.

Dinner at Leonard's

On Wednesday evening, Rick walked across the campus to the Varsity Apartments. This sprawling complex, covering several square blocks, is made up of a series of two-story buildings, each containing eight apartments—four on each floor. Rick found building "H," and entered the lobby. He checked the mailboxes and found one with the name, Dr. Gerald A. Leonard, and pushed the intercom button above it.

He half hoped that no one would answer. After Tim's remark on Sunday night, he wondered if he should have agreed to this dinner meeting. He thought that Leonard might forget, but he had mentioned it again to Rick after class on Wednesday.

"That you, Rick?" Dr. Leonard's voice came over the intercom.

"Yes."

"Come on up. I'm in Number 5, at the top of the stairs."

By the time Rick got to the upper hall, a door opened, and Dr. Leonard stepped out to greet him. He was wearing his usual jeans, an open neck shirt with a pullover sweater, and an apron.

As Rick shook hands, his eyes dropped to the apron, and Dr. Leonard noticed it.

"When you live alone, you have to do everything," he explained.

"Didn't realize you lived alone," Rick said, somewhat embarrassed.

"I'll explain that later," Leonard said. "You just find a chair, and I'll finish dinner."

It was a one-bedroom apartment, bath, living room, dining room, and a small kitchen off to one end.

The living room looked more like a storage room in a furniture warehouse. It was crammed with furniture, plants, and bookcases on every wall. And over everything were books—on the floor, on tables, and even an open book on the sofa.

"Wow, the books!" Rick exclaimed. "I've never seen so many in one house. You must have more than the library."

"I do have more in my field than the library," Dr. Leonard called back from the kitchen.

Rick walked around and examined a few of the titles. Most of them were on psychology, but others were on literature, history, and a number on philosophy. Under one pile of books he saw the familiar edges of an open Bible. "At least he reads the Bible," Rick thought to himself.

He also noticed a picture sitting on the bookcase. It was of Leonard when he was much younger, and with him was a very beautiful young girl. It looked to Rick as if it had been taken at a high school prom.

Leonard shuttled back and forth between the kitchen and the dining room table, and then after a few minutes announced, "I guess we're ready. You take this chair, and I'll sit in this one next to the kitchen."

It was an excellent meal, and Rick thoroughly enjoyed it. There were broiled steaks, a green salad, and a big bowl of green lima beans. As Rick took another helping of the beans, he said, "How did you know these were my favorites?"

"I didn't, just lucked out," Leonard said. "When I have guests, I make what I like, and they have to eat it, or go without. It's much more fun cooking for someone than eating alone. I eat out a lot."

"Have you always lived alone?" Rick asked.

"No, but we'll get to that later," Leonard said.

Rick changed the subject, and they talked about items of mutual interest around school. As they talked, Rick began to relax and enjoy himself. Leonard proved to be an excellent conversationalist. He was obviously well-read, and could talk on any subject Rick might bring up.

After dinner, Rick helped Leonard clear the table and put the dishes in the dishwasher. When they returned to the living room, Leonard went to a large chair which looked like his favorite, and Rick settled down on one end of the sofa.

"Now, let's get back to our class discussion,"

Leonard began. "Seems to me that you were talking about some absolute standards of right and wrong. Am I right?"

"Yeah. I guess so," Rick said hesitantly.

"You were objecting to my statement that sexual standards were culturally defined, if I'm not mistaken."

"I was merely trying to suggest that some things are always right, and some things are always wrong in every country and every culture," Rick said. "Don't you believe that?"

"Name one universal wrong," Leonard said.

Rick thought for a minute. "Well, what about stealing—taking something that doesn't belong to you is always wrong. Everybody sees that as a wrong."

"Let's say that there is a woman who has a little baby. She has no food to feed that baby, and no money with which to buy food. But she loves the baby. Is it right for the mother to look after her child?"

"Sure."

"Even if she steals some food to feed it?"

"But couldn't she find some other way?" Rick asked.

"Aw, now you're changing the assumptions. I'm assuming there is no other way."

"I guess maybe she shouldn't let the child starve," Rick said, "but the Bible says in Exodus 12, 'Thou shalt not steal.'"

"Then you're admitting that stealing is all right if she really loves the child?"

Rick didn't answer.

"Let's try another," Leonard said. "Suppose you and a girl were cast on some desert island together. You found each other attractive, but there was no way to get married—no way to get a license, no way to get a preacher. Would it be O.K. for you to have sex with the girl?"

"Those are unusual situations," Rick said.

"Yes, I know, but if you are going to make universal laws, they must be universal. If you can break them in one case, they are not universal."

"But the Bible says, 'Thou shalt not com—' "

"I know, 'Thou shalt not commit adultery.' That is found in Exodus 20:4. And incidentally, 'Thou shalt not steal,' is found in Exodus 20:15."

"Sorry. Doesn't that make it a universal law?"

"It was given to a specific people at a specific time. Just because it worked for them, doesn't mean that it will work for us."

"Are you against all law?" Rick asked. "How could a society exist without laws?"

"That's not the point at all. I'm talking in both of my examples about a higher law—the law of love. This law puts some flexibility in all of those other laws, and makes them more palatable to all of us."

"Did you always believe like this?" Rick asked, trying to take the heat off himself.

Dr. Leonard's eyes dropped, and Rick knew instantly he had touched a responsive spot. Finally, he looked up and said, "Maybe I should tell you something about myself so you know where I'm coming from. I grew up in a strict fundamentalist home."

"You mean your parents were Christians?" Rick

asked, in a surprised voice.

"I thought that would surprise you," Leonard said. "Yes, I went to Sunday School and church from the time I was a baby. I don't think I ever missed Sunday School until I went away to college."

"Then what happened?" Rick asked, now genuinely interested.

"Nothing different than happens to many good, church-going boys who must face the real issues of life for the first time. I've watched students like you come and go, and many of them are the same. They come to college, just like you, full of faith and high ideals, but by the time they've been here a little while, they begin to question everything they have ever been taught."

Rick's mind flashed back over the past three weeks, and he knew exactly what Leonard was saying. "And that's what happened to you?"

"I had only been in college a few days when I went to see a professor about an assignment. He was a philosophy teacher, and I had some question about an early Greek philosopher. I was totally ignorant about philosophy, and went to seek an answer to an honest question. The professor was young, handsome, brilliant, and very articulate. He could answer my questions in such a way that I began to hang on to his every word. Whatever he said was the gospel truth to me, if you pardon the pun."

"Did he question your faith?"

"Not directly. He just planted a seed of doubt here and there. He suggested outside reading assignments which agreed with his way of thinking, and he always seemed to ask me questions which I couldn't answer. He became my idol. I took a course from him the next quarter, and when it came time for me to select an advisor, I immediately selected him. Then, under his influence, I selected philosophy as an undergraduate major, and spent many, many hours under his influence."

"Sounds like you got a lot of personalized instruction," Rick said.

"No one could have had more attention than I did. But I soon found myself comparing everything he said to what I had learned at home and church. When I went home for a weekend, I spent my time arguing with my parents, and questioning everything the pastor said. As the arguments got louder and longer, I quit going home excepting on vacations, and quit going to church. I quit reading the Bible, and completely changed the lifestyle which I had known at home. And do you know why?"

Rick shook his head.

"Because that professor really cared about me. For the first time in my life, I felt someone valued me as a person. I was just an average kid—nothing special about me, so no teacher in high school ever went out of his or her way for me. My parents loved me, but mainly because I was their child, and parents are supposed to love their children. My pastor never really knew I existed. I was only one of the 'young people'. For the first time in my life I felt that someone really loved me. He lived alone, so when he asked me if I wanted to live with him, I immediately accepted and moved into his apartment."

"But I don't understand how anyone could have had so much influence over the thinking of another," Rick said.

"College teachers have a profound influence over the thinking of their students—more than either of us care to admit. You think your faith is strong, but little by little, it can be eroded by a question here and a remark there. You can never be the same after you have had Psych under me. It is only a question of which direction you will go. I'm not really asking that you believe as I do now, but you'd better get some solid answers to your questions or you may find yourself changing radically. If I can shake your God off His throne, then you don't have a very sure God."

"But I don't have much of a chance when everyone I meet—students, professors, roommates—everyone seems bent on making me change," Rick said.

"If your faith is half as great as you say it is, it can stand anything I or anyone else can dish out around here. I'm going to personally see that you leave this school with some firm beliefs, either in a new pragmatic philosophy, or your own. Everyone needs a philosophy of life, something to live by, and I want to help you develop yours."

The room was quiet as Leonard allowed Rick to think about his words. Then in a softer tone, Leonard said, "Believing in something is always costly."

"How's that?" Rick asked.

"You asked me about living alone. I didn't always plan to live by myself. I hoped to get married once."

"To that girl," Rick said, pointing to the picture on the bookcase.

"Yes, that's the one. We grew up together. She was brought up in a Christian home too, but when I changed, she couldn't accept it. She couldn't understand my new philosophy of life, or my new lifestyle. So she quit me, and even today she remains true to her church. What I believed cost me that marriage, but I had to do it. Come to think of it, what she believed also cost her a marriage, because she is still single. One simply must be true to one's self."

Rick got up. "Thanks, Dr. Leonard. Thanks a lot. The dinner was great, and you really made me think, but I've got some thinking to do on my own now. Maybe we can talk again later. I needed this more than you will ever know."

"Sure, Rick. I know this has been quite a load to throw at a new Freshman, but you looked like someone who could take it. I wanted to start you to thinking. If you ever need to get away from the dorm, you're always welcome here."

Rick thanked his host again, and they shook hands. When he stepped out into the night, there was a bright harvest moon, and the heavens were studded with a million stars. There was just the first hint of fall chill in the air.

As he walked alone, Rick looked up into the sky and said, "Lord, I need You. I really need You. Please reveal Yourself to me in a new way. I thought I believed in You before, but now I'm not certain. I'm not even sure You exist any more. If You do, and if everything I've been taught these years is true, please make Yourself real to me again."

And the rest of the way back to the dorm, Rick found himself softly singing an old church hymn,

> "*And He walks with me,*
> *And He talks with me,*
> *And He tells me I am His own . . .*"

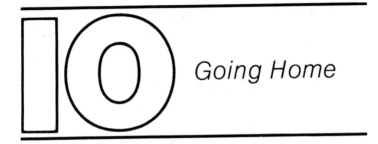

Going Home

Once again, when Rick got back to the dorm after classes on Friday, he found a letter waiting from Ann. He took it to his room, and stretched out on the bed and began to read.

As in the previous letters, it was filled with news of friends, and familiar places. As he read on, some old feelings began to reappear. At first it was just a sense of nostalgia, but then it became a real longing for home and everything it represented to him. Everything seemed so simple and beautiful in the world which Ann was describing. He longed to feel again that total faith in himself and in the future he had known in high school.

"If I could just see them all again, even for a few hours, maybe I would feel better," he said to himself.

Rick suddenly dropped the letter and sat up in bed. He looked at his watch. It was still only 3:30.

"Why *can't* I go home this weekend?" he asked himself. "I could be there by 7:30 or 8:00, and that would be time enough for me to see Ann, and maybe even see some of the old gang."

When Rick left home, he had promised himself and all of his friends that he would stay at school for six weeks before coming home. It hadn't occurred to him that he might want to come home before that time. After all, he had been at camp for almost three months, and hadn't even thought about going home.

Rick threw a few things into a gym bag, took a sport coat and slacks out of the closet, and headed for the door. He stopped once again and looked back at the pile of books on his bed. "Won't look at them anyway," he muttered to himself, as he turned and went out the door, leaving them all behind.

As he turned off First Street and onto Highway 169, it seemed that even the car sensed his excitement. He hadn't had it out on the highway since coming to school, so it seemed good to open it up again.

It was unusually warm for October, so he turned down the car windows, allowing the warm autumn air to blow through his hair. The golden oaks and red maples along the river bluffs were set against a backdrop of bright blue sky. The world was warm and beautiful, and Rick felt the same way, for the first time in three weeks.

As he approached the Cities, the traffic became heavier, so it was after 8 o'clock before he pulled up into the driveway. He jumped out of the car and took two steps at a time up to the back door. He was about to reach for his keys as he had done so many times before, when he remembered that he had left them at home. He had decided he really didn't need them anymore if he was leaving home.

But it did seem odd to be ringing the doorbell in his own home. It sorta made him feel like a stranger. He could see the flicker of the TV in the living room, so he knew someone was home.

He pushed the button again, then heard footsteps coming toward the door.

"Rick, what are you doing home?" his ten-year-old brother asked.

"Hi, Peanut," Rick answered, "where's the folks?"

"You didn't answer my question," Bill said, closing the door behind them.

"Just because I wanted to come home. O.K?" Rick answered, sounding annoyed.

"Yeah, sure, I guess so," Bill said, "but Heather ain't going to like it."

"What's she got to do with it?" Rick asked, throwing his coat on a chair, and his gym bag on the kitchen table. "What's the big deal about a fellow coming back to his own home?"

"You don't have to get sore about it," Bill said, obviously hurt.

"I'm not sore, Peanut. It's just that I've had a long hard day, and I guess I expected a little more enthusiasm about my first visit home. Now, what about Heather, and where are the folks?"

"Mom and Dad are at some church party. Said they would be back about eleven, but told me to be in bed by ten. And Heather—she's going to be coming home from the game any minute with six screaming girls. And they're going to stay here all night! That's why they need your room."

"You mean I leave here for only three weeks, and my sister has taken over my room?"

"Sorry," Bill said, shrugging his shoulders. "Wanta watch TV?"

"I have to call Ann first," Rick said.

Bill went back to the living room, and Rick dialed Ann's number on the kitchen phone. The line was busy, so he waited for a few minutes and tried again. This time it was Ann's father who answered.

"Hello, Mr. Thornton. This is Rick."

"Rick! What a surprise. Where are you?"

"Home."

"What are you doing home?"

"Seems I've been asked that before. I just decided to come home for the weekend."

"That's great, but Ann will sure be disappointed that she missed you."

"Why, isn't Ann home?" Rick asked, trying not to sound too disappointed.

"No, she isn't. I'm sorry, Rick. I'm sure she would have stayed home if she had known you were coming, but she went with some of the church kids to a retreat at camp. They left right after school tonight, and won't be back until Sunday afternoon."

After a moment of silence, Rick said, "Well, I guess I can't blame her. After all, she didn't know I was coming. Who went?"

"I think she rode with Tom. I overheard her say to her mother that she and Lorrie would be riding with Tom and Dan in Tom's car."

"O.K., thanks, Mr. Thornton. You can tell her I called."

Rick stood for a moment holding the receiver before putting it back on the hook.

"Tom," Rick muttered. "So she went with Tom, did she?"

He went to the living room and dropped on the sofa, then began to stare at the TV without being conscious of what he was watching.

"What a bummer," he thought. "I leave home for three weeks, and everyone forgets me. My folks are gone, I'm in my sister's way, and Ann is too busy having fun to stay home."

He began to think about camp, and the group now seated around the big fireplace in the basement of the dining hall. He had been there many times before, so he knew exactly how it was. And that was the trouble, he knew how it was, so he felt sorry for himself that he was missing it.

About 9:30, the back door opened, and the house was invaded by six tenth-grade girls carrying sleeping bags, curling irons, hair dryers, and overnight cases. When Heather came into the living room and spotted Rick, she let out a cry. "Rick, you aren't supposed to be home this weekend!"

"But I am," he said, not taking his eyes off the TV.

"But you can't do this to me! I'm having a slumber party, and I need your room."

"So I've heard," Rick answered, still being noncommittal about it all.

"Didn't I tell you she'd be mad?" Bill said looking up from his position on the floor.

"You'll just have to leave," Heather said defiantly as the other girls gathered around her all glaring at Rick as if he had committed a crime.

"I'm not leaving. This is my home as much as it is yours," Rick answered.

"But I can't change my plans now. They're all here!" Heather sounded as if she were about to cry.

"Don't get so uptight," Rick said, a smile breaking across his face. "Go ahead and use my room, I'm staying with Bill."

"Let's go, girls," Heather said, motioning to the others to follow her. "One brother is bad enough when you're trying to have a party, but two is just too much!"

The girls followed Heather toward the bedrooms, and Bill and Rick turned their attention back to the TV. When the next commercial came on, Bill got up from the floor, and sat down next to Rick.

"I'm glad to have you home," Bill said, moving closer to his brother.

"And it's good to be here with you, Peanuts," Rick said, reaching over and messing up Bill's hair. "Dorms are noisy, but they're nothing like having a little brother around."

"Gee, thanks. I think," Bill said grinning.

After the commercial, the Western resumed, and Rick became so involved in the story that he hardly noticed the screams and giggles coming from the bedrooms and kitchen as the slumber party progressed. Eventually Bill fell asleep, and Rick pulled his brother's head down on his lap to make him more comfortable.

It was about eleven when the Ericksons came home.

"Why in the world are you home?" Mrs. Erickson said as she ran over and gave Rick a big hug.

"Just 'cause I wanted to be," Rick answered. "Do I have to have a reason?"

"Of course not. It's just that we weren't expecting you," she answered.

"I've noticed," Rick said, almost under his breath.

"Hi, Dad," Rick said as Mr. Erickson came into the room.

"Rick! What . . ."

"I know, what am I doing home?" Rick interrupted. "Several people have already asked that, and I'm beginning to wonder myself. I just came home because I wanted to come home. After living here for eighteen years, it takes a little time getting used to the idea of being away. O.K.?"

"Sure, Son," his dad said warmly, "we're glad you want to come home. I hope it will always be that way."

After a few minutes of general chitchat, Mrs. Erickson asked the question which every mother has asked every son who has ever gone to college since the beginning of higher education. "And how do you like college?"

And Rick's answer was equally predictable. "Aw, it's O.K., I guess. It's sure different from high school."

She didn't pursue the subject any further, and Rick was glad for that because he really didn't know how he felt about college. It was too early to tell, and there were too many questions going through his mind right now.

"I suppose Bill told you that your room is occupied?"

"Yeah, we've been through that. I'll sleep in Bill's upper bunk. Come to think of it, it's time to go there right now. Come on, Bill," Rick said, shaking the sleeping form on his lap. "Let's hit the sack."

"Oh, by the way," Rick's mother said, "your father and I have to be at church for a prayer breakfast at 7:30 tomorrow morning. I suspect you can find something to eat when you get up. We'll talk tomorrow."

"Yeah, we'll talk tomorrow . . . sometime," Rick answered.

But there was little time for family talk on Saturday. When Rick awoke, Heather and her friends had taken over the living room and were watching television. Bill was still asleep, and his parents had gone to their breakfast.

After eating some cold cereal and drinking a glass of milk, Rick decided to drive around town to see if he could find some of his old friends. He soon discovered this was more difficult than he had anticipated. Some were away to school and had not come home for the weekend. Several were with the youth group at the Retreat, and one had even enlisted in the Navy.

Rick went by his old high school, and then started North on Nicollet Ave. When he got to 86th Street, he could see the golden arches of a McDonalds on the left side of the street. Seeing them reminded him that Larry was probably at work, so he swung in to check it out.

When Larry saw Rick at the counter, he called from the kitchen, "Hey, Rick, why don't you find a booth and wait around. I'm due for a break in about ten minutes."

As Rick sipped a Coke, he thought about how different this day was developing than he had anticipated. He had planned on spending the day with Ann, but she was gone. He looked forward to seeing his folks, but they were too busy with church activities to really have time for him, and most of the familiar faces around town seemed to have vanished.

Rick's thoughts went to a novel which he was reading for his English class. It was Thomas Wolfe's *You Can't Go Home Again*, and Rick was beginning to understand what Wolfe was trying to say.

It was good to see Larry again, even though they had not been the closest of friends. In a situation like this, almost anyone he knew seemed good to see. Larry had decided to live at home and go to the local community college. He had been working at McDonalds throughout his last year of High School, so he decided to stay on until something better came along.

But even as they talked, Rick sensed a strangeness. It was more difficult to talk to Larry now. They had no common school activities to discuss, and Larry was totally involved in church activities, and couldn't really understand Rick's new world. Larry went to classes at the college and then left again, so he had no ties to the college community. After Larry's break, he went back to work. Rick did some more cruising, and then headed back home.

Mr. and Mrs. Erickson were there when he arrived, but both Bill and Heather were going to friends' houses. Mrs. Erickson made some sandwiches for the three, and they had a pleasant time of conversation around the kitchen table.

They were still at the table when the phone rang and Mrs. Erickson answered.

"Hello. Yes, Pastor. Yes, I'm sure we can manage that. Rick surprised us and came home, but I'm sure that won't take long."

She hung up the phone and turned back toward the table. "That was the Pastor. He wondered if we could go over and set up the Sunday School rooms again. We didn't do that after last night's party, and the janitor is sick today. You won't mind, will you Rick, if we leave a little while? It shouldn't take long."

"Naw, go ahead. I'll just watch TV till you come home."

Rick went into the living room, turned on the TV, and laid back on the Lazy Boy. He started to watch football but soon fell asleep. It was halftime when he awakened, and discovered he was still alone in the house. This time he turned off the TV, and laid down again. He wasn't sleepy now, so his mind began to wander.

He began to think about the invitation to a Saturday night party which he had received, but refused. Now he wished he had stayed at Southern, and he wished he was going to the party. "At least I would feel wanted there," he thought.

And once again, as he had done the day before,

he looked at his watch and said to himself, "Why not? Why can't I go to that party? I've got time to get there, and nobody around here will miss me!"

Rick jumped up, went to the kitchen, found a piece of paper, and quickly wrote:

> *Dear Mom and Dad:*
> *Since no one is around here that I wanted to see, I decided to go back to school. Got a lot of studying I can do this weekend. I'll be back in two weeks.*
>
> Love,
> Rick

He went to the bedroom, stuffed his clothes back in the gym bag, and left the house.

And all the way back to Southern, he thought about spending another evening with Kandi.

Another Party

The invitation to this party had come when Rick had bumped into Kandi in the Student Union on Wednesday.

"Well, there's the crusader," she had said, pushing her way through the cafeteria line to where he was standing.

"What do you mean by that?" Rick asked.

"You must not have read the DAILY this morning."

"Nope, haven't had time."

"Buy me a Coke, and I'll let you read mine," she said.

Her smile, and the way she threw her long hair over one shoulder made Rick forget that he was supposed to be mad at her.

"Go find a table," he said. "I'll bring the Cokes."

"O.K., now what's in the DAILY?" he asked, pulling up a chair beside her.

"Right here on page one it says,

> An Anti-liquor rally will be held in the Holmgren dorm activity room next Monday evening at 8:00. It was organized by an ad hoc group of students to show opposition to the bill before the State Legislature which would legalize drinking in the dorms. Featured speakers for the evening will be four students: Rick Erickson, Freshman; Gary Gill, Sophomore; Jim Elliott, Junior; and Bill Lawrence, Senior.

"Want to hear more?"

"Naw, I've heard too much already," Rick responded.

"You really do take your religion seriously, don't you?" Kandi said. The question sounded authentic, but her voice showed skepticism.

"Seems like we've been through this before," Rick said.

"What do you know about liquor?' Kandi asked.

"Not much, I guess, except what I see and read."

"Then how can you fight something you don't know anything about?"

"There are some things you just know are right or wrong without experiencing them," Rick answered.

"Tell you what," Kandi said, "I'm having a little group of friends over to the apartment Saturday night. Everyone knows where you stand after today's paper, so why don't you come over and let them tell you their side of the story. It's only fair that you hear it before you make your speech."

"I'm not sure I can trust you. Remember what happened the last time I came to a party at your house."

"That has nothing to do with the subject at hand. The question is, are you man enough to hear the other side of the question, or are you so closed-minded that you can't stand to hear the other side?"

Rick could tell that Kandi was serious, and a challenge like this was hard to refuse, but he had decided to stay away from her place. "Why invite temptation?" he had told himself.

"No, thanks," Rick said. "I'm sure your crowd couldn't tell me anything I haven't already heard or read."

"You're even more pig-headed than I thought," Kandi said. "Don't blame me if your little speech bombs out next week."

"I'll take my chances," Rick had said.

Rick had gone away from the encounter with Kandi last Wednesday feeling rather good about the firm way he had handled the situation, but now his mood had changed, and he was headed back to Southern, back to Kandi's party, and somehow it all seemed so right. He hadn't found what he was seeking at home, so maybe he could find it there.

He arrived in Mill Town about 7:30, so went directly to Kandi's apartment. She didn't seem at all surprised when he came to the door. She acted as if she had been expecting him all along, and soon he was comfortable—more comfortable than he had been any time since coming to school.

By 8:30, there were about twenty students crowded into the little two-room apartment. As each one came, he or she went to the kitchen and got a bottle of beer from the refrigerator, and with some mellow jazz playing in the background, they gathered in small groups around the room.

Rick was beginning to think that Kandi had forgotten why she had invited him to this party when he heard her say, "Hey gang . . ." She stopped and turned off the stereo.

The talking began to die down, and Kandi said, "Gang, most of you have met Rick Erickson by now."

Rick felt his face begin to turn red as all eyes turned toward him.

"And you've read in the DAILY about the rally to be held next week. Rick here is one of the speakers, and he needs some material, so I've asked him to come over tonight so that you can let him know how you feel about drinking in the dorms. Rick, come over here and sit by me so that everyone can see you, and you can see everybody."

Kandi was sitting on her desk, and moved over so that Rick could sit beside her. Those in the room who were standing, either found a chair, or sat down on the floor.

"Now," Kandi continued, "what about it—should the legislature allow liquor in the dorms? What do you think, Don?" she asked, pointing to a rather tall, thin art student.

"I can't see why there needs to be a law either way," Don said. "If we are renting a room, it's just like renting an apartment. We can't help it that the state happens to be the landlord. As long as we pay our room and board, that's our home, and nobody should be allowed to tell us what to do there."

"Right," said another fellow who was already on his third beer, and gave evidence of having had something stronger before coming to the party. "I say, it's high time they start treating us like adults instead of kindergarten kids."

"Did it ever occur to you that there are some in that dorm who don't drink, and who find it objectionable?" Rick asked.

"Are you kidding?" he answered, "I don't know anyone under twenty-five who doesn't drink."

"I don't," Rick answered.

"Have you ever tried it?"

"No."

"Here, have a drink," the fellow said, standing up and setting his half-filled bottle on the desk by Rick.

Everyone laughed, except Rick.

"Come on, you're a man now," he said, standing directly in front of him.

Rick felt himself beginning to lose his cool. "What right have you to force your habits on me?" he said standing up so that he could look the fellow in the eye.

"I feel it is my moral obligation to make you a member of the human race," he answered.

As Rick took one step forward, the other fellow mistook his movements for an attack, so he grabbed him by the shirt with one hand, doubled up his other fist, and let him have a solid whack across the mouth.

Rick fell backwards into Kandi's arms. Several of the girls screamed, and then there was dead silence in the room as everyone waited for the next move.

Blood began to ooze from a cut on Rick's upper lip. He opened his eyes in time to see the fellow lunge at him once more, "I can't stand these pious, smart-mouths," he was saying.

Kandi turned, with Rick still in her arms, in such a way that the fellow was caught off-balance, and his left hook simply went into thin air. Two of the other fellows jumped up and grabbed the first fellow in time to keep him from taking another swing.

Rick stood to his feet and turned to Kandi. "I think I have heard enough," he said. "It's time for me to go home."

"Don't go, Rick," Kandi pleaded.

Her voice sounded so sincere that Rick took a second look. "Why not? I'm not sure I've exactly enjoyed your friends," he said.

"Please, don't go," Kandi said again, "I'm sorry about the fight."

Rick took one last look at Kandi, and then, as he felt a drop of blood fall on his hand, he turned, and without another word headed for the door.

But as he opened the door, he was greeted by an unexpected sight. There standing, ready to come in, were two local police officers.

"O.K., fellow, where do you think you're going?" one of them said as each one grabbed one of Rick's arms.

"Police!" someone shouted.

"O.K., everyone," the police said, leading Rick back into the room. "Let's see everyone's ID's."

They began to check drivers' licenses one by one, and those who were over 19 were separated on one side of the room. When they got to Rick, he said, "But I wasn't drinking . . . honest."

"With a lip like that, I suppose you were baby-sitting?" he said with a sneer. "From the looks of this room everyone was drinking."

Rick saw the futility of the discussion, and pulled out his driver's license.

"O.K., over there with the rest of the juveniles," the officer said.

The rest of the evening was a nightmare for Rick. He tried to make himself believe he was dreaming, but each time the hard reality of the situation would come back. Those who were under nineteen were taken to the police station, fingerprinted and locked up.

Rick sat down on the edge of the bunk and put his head in his hands. The bleeding had stopped, but he could feel his lip beginning to swell. His mind began to race madly from one thought to another in wild confusion. He had never been inside a jail, not even for a visit, and here he was, an inmate. The whole thing was so absurd that he began to chuckle to himself.

"What's the matter, you cracking up?" a voice asked.

Rick hadn't been aware of someone else in the cell with him. He looked over to the next bunk, and in the dim light of the room, he could make out the face of one of the fellows who had been at the party. Rick remembered that he had not been introduced to him, and that he had remained quiet throughout the evening.

"I said, what's so funny?" he repeated.

"Just thinking . . . thinking how odd it is for me to be in here," Rick said.

"First time?"

"Yeah. How about you?"

"Naw, guess you can say I kinda feel at home. I do remember the first time, though."

"How old were you?"

"About nine. I ripped off some candy from the corner store, and the old man who ran it thought he would teach me a lesson and had me arrested."

"Sounds as if it didn't help."

"Naw. At fourteen I was sent to the Juvenile Detention Center for armed robbery, and from there I went to a boys' ranch which is something like a jail."

"Sounds real mixed up," Rick said, for want of something better to say. "What did your parents say about all of this?"

"What parents?" the boy snapped.

"Sorry."

"About all they did for me was to bring me into the world, and that wasn't a favor."

Eventually both boys laid back in their bunks and between some wild mixed-up dreams, Rick got a little sleep. It was early the next morning when he heard the sound of a key in the cell door. The same officer who had arrested them the night before, came into the room and said, "We're letting you fellows go now, but you will have to appear in court next Friday. We've called the dean, and he has assured us that he will have you here for that appointment."

Rick and his cell mate walked out into the lobby, and as they did, a figure got up from one of the chairs and came toward them.

"Kandi," Rick exclaimed. "What are you doing here?"

"What does it look like? I always sleep in a chair in the lobby of the police station," she answered. "I came to take you home."

"Haven't you caused me enough trouble for one day?" Rick said, pulling his arm back from her outstretched hand.

"Is that all the thanks I get for spending the night in a chair waiting for you! Come on, I've got your jacket."

This time Kandi simply grabbed his arm and began to lead him toward the door.

Rick was too tired and emotionally drained to argue, and he didn't feel up to walking back to the dorm.

Kandi had found Rick's keys in the pocket of his jacket, and had driven his car to the station, so they got into it and headed toward her apartment. He was about to park in front and let her out when she said, "You're not going anywhere until I make you some breakfast."

"I really think I should go back to the dorm," Rick said, as if trying to convince himself.

"What's the matter, you afraid of me?"

"No, I'm afraid of me and what I might do," Rick answered.

"But Marcia is gone, and I'll be all alone," Kandi pleaded.

"That's why I'm afraid," Rick answered.

12 Exit—Stage Left

When Rick got back to his room, he found it just the way he had left it on Friday evening. Apparently Bert had not been in either Friday or Saturday night. Neither he, nor Marcia, had been to the party, and no one, not even Kandi seemed to know where they were.

The experiences of the past twenty-four hours made Rick feel much older than the boy who had left on Friday evening. As he thought about these experiences, his feelings ranged from guilt, to pleasure, to anger, and back again to guilt. Always back to guilt. He tried to tell himself that nothing had been his fault, that he had been a victim of circumstances, but still he knew that he had made the decision to come back to Mill City, and to go to the party.

He tried to convince himself that he had done nothing wrong, but after eighteen years of moral and ethical training in church, he knew that something was wrong, very wrong, and that made him feel even more guilty.

And he was also angry—angry at the kid who had punched him and tried to make him take a drink, and angry at the officer who wouldn't believe his story. He thought about the upcoming rally, and was more convinced than ever that he should fight the use of liquor in the dorms. He would hate to see a repeat of last night in the dormitories.

As Rick was leaving the cafeteria at noon, he met Wayne Larson who was just coming back from church.

"How's the speech coming?" Wayne asked.

"Been working on it," Rick responded.

"The committee is getting together about three to plan strategy for the rally," Wayne said. "Let's meet in the lounge."

"O.K., see you there," Rick answered.

By three, Rick had finished a draft of his speech. He had gone to the library to get some more statistics, and was quite pleased with the arguments which he had developed. His experience in high school debate was coming in handy now.

The committee members met at three as planned. They reported that the resident counselor had agreed to act as Master of Ceremonies for the rally. The plan was for him to introduce each member of the board and administration first, then visiting legislators, and finally the four student speakers. Each speaker would be allowed about ten minutes for his presentation, and this would be followed by a period of questions and answers. When everyone was satisfied with the plan, the meeting broke up, and Rick went back toward his room.

He had the key in hand, ready to unlock the door when he noticed that it was already partly open. Thinking Bert was back, he pushed the door wide open, and then stopped short. Instead of Bert, there were two uniformed policemen in the room, and everything was in disarray.

"Sorry, kid, you can't come in here," one of the officers said.

"But this is my room," Rick responded.

"It's also Bert Kemp's room, isn't it?" the police asked.

"Sure, but why are you here? What are you looking for?"

"We're with the State Narcotics Division, and we have a search warrant for this room," the other officer said.

Other students began to gather around Rick and peer over his shoulders into the room.

"If this is his room, we had better ask him a few questions," one officer said to the other, pointing to Rick.

They motioned for Rick to come into the room, and then shut the door in the face of the gathering crowd. "Have a chair while we finish our search," the officer said.

Rick stared in utter disbelief as they went through everything in the room. They searched every drawer, every piece of clothing, and even felt the mattresses for any suspicious lumps. When they seemed satisfied they could find nothing, they turned their attention to Rick. One officer took out a pad, and began taking notes while the other asked the questions.

"Have you ever witnessed your roommate using any kind of drugs?" the officer began.

"We hardly ever see each other, so how could I?" Rick answered.

"Have you ever smelled any suspicious odors on him when he came into the room?"

"I don't even know what drugs smell like, so how could I?" Rick answered.

"We have reason to believe that Mr. Kemp has been pushing drugs on this campus. If so, it's hard to believe that his own roommate would not have seen something suspicious."

"As far as I know, he's just a normal student who is out for a good time, and parties a lot," Rick said.

"These parties . . . do you know where he goes for these parties?"

"Sure, some of them," Rick said, but as soon as he had said it, he realized who he was implicating.

"Tell us where!" the officer said, while the other one held his pencil ready to take down whatever Rick said.

"I don't exactly know . . . " Rick stammered.

"But you just said you did," the officer said. "You might just as well tell us what you know. We'll find out sooner or later anyway."

"I know he has been in an apartment downtown several times," Rick said, still trying to be evasive.

"Where downtown?"

"In an apartment on South 5th. 405 South 5th, Apartment 5."

"Thanks, that will be all for now," the officer said.

"Where is Bert? What has happened to him?" Rick asked. "I haven't seen him since Friday morning."

"We have him in custody, along with his girl friend," the officer said, turning to leave. "I wouldn't wait up for him—not for a few days," he said as he went out the door.

As soon as the officers were gone, the door flew open, and the room filled with curious students. Everyone was asking questions, and it seemed each one had a different theory about what was wrong with Bert. No one, including his friend Paul, had seen Bert since about noon on Friday.

Both Wayne and Randy were part of the group in Rick's room, and when the crowd began to thin out, they reminded Rick that it was about time for the Bible study. In all the confusion, Rick had forgotten about it, and was really in no mood to go, but decided it would be one way for him to find a little peace of mind.

He had difficulty concentrating on the lesson, and contributed very little to the discussion. When the prayer time came, he spent most of the time praying silently for himself rather than listening to the others' prayers. They all remembered Bert, and asked God to do a miracle in his life. Rick prayed for Bert too, but somehow his words sounded hollow in his own ears. He wondered if others noticed it.

After the prayer time, they sat around and talked for a little while, and during that conversation, Randy said to Rick,"Say, do you ever see that girl you introduced me to in the Union? Think her name was Kandi."

"Aw—yes. Why?" Rick said, trying to sound casual.

"Well, she has talked to me several times in the Union, and boy, is she ever full of questions!"

"About what?"

"About God, the Bible, and why I don't do this or that," Randy said. "Somebody must be making her think, and I wondered if maybe it was you."

"Hardly," Rick said, his mind flashing back to the previous night. He felt himself turning red, and hoped no one would notice.

"I really think you should talk to her," Randy said. "She seems to like you, and she is ready to do some serious thinking."

"If you say so," Rick said, getting up. "But I don't think I can do her much good."

He left before the conversation could go any further.

There was still no new information about Bert when Rick left for the rally on Monday night. He obviously had not been back to the room, and Rick had not seen him, Kandi, or Marcia on campus that day.

When he arrived at the lounge, he was surprised to find the room almost full. When he stuck his head in the door, he saw Wayne up front motioning to him, so he worked his way through the crowd toward the front of the room.

"You're supposed to sit up there," Wayne said, pointing to the five chairs on the little raised platform.

"Can't I just stay here until it's my turn?" Rick

asked.

"No, they want you up there. It's easier to throw tomatoes at you that way," he said, chuckling.

"Gee, thanks a lot," Rick said. "You make a fellow feel real good."

The others were already in their places, so Rick took the only empty chair on the platform. He began to look over the crowd hoping to see some familiar faces. The fellows from the Bible study were there, and he recognized several from the Saturday night's party, but most of the students were strangers to him. The only faculty member he recognized was Dr. Leonard, sitting near the front.

When it was time to begin, the Master of Ceremonies stepped to the mike, and the crowd became quiet.

"As most of you know," he began, "there is a law in this state which prohibits the possession of alcoholic beverages in the dorms at any of our state colleges. It seems that there are those who feel this is an outmoded law, and should be repealed. So there is a bill before the state legislature this session which would do just that. As you can imagine, it has caused quite a bit of discussion throughout the state, and a number of students here at Southern thought that our state legislators needed to know what the students think about it. So, that is why we have invited our representatives from this area to be our guests tonight.

"First, I would like to have you meet Dr. Albert Swanson. He is the representative from the fifth district which includes the campus. Dr. Swanson, will you please stand."

A middle-aged, well-dressed individual stood, and the students applauded politely.

"Also from the fourth district, which includes the towns West of here, from which a large portion of our students come, is Fred Finholm. Mr. Finholm, would you please stand." This time a ruddy-faced man in his forties with jeans and an open-neck flannel shirt arose. Once again the students applauded—somewhat more vigorously this time.

"Now, ladies and gentlemen, we have representatives from each of the four classes here at Southern. We have asked each one to address you for about ten minutes. At the close of all of their speeches, we will allow time for questions and answers, and any other discussion which you might have."

The leader then introduced each one of the speakers beginning with the one from the Senior class, and going on down to the Freshman class. That meant that Rick was last.

When it was his turn, he stepped to the mike, cleared his throat, and began to read from his prepared notes.

"A recent Gallup poll shows alcoholism to be the nation's number one problem among the 20 to 40-year-old bracket, and that 76 percent of those who consider themselves to be alcoholic state that they became that way during their college years.

"No one is so naive as to believe that keeping liquor out of the dorms will stop everyone from drinking, but why should we openly condone making everyone's room his own private tavern?

"Further, the dorms are owned by the state, and therefore the property of the people—the vast majority of which are still non-drinkers. Why make them a party to the development of future alcoholics?

"And there are those who find it repulsive to see others drink. We pay good money to live in these dorms. They are our homes for nine months of the year. If we don't drink, we should have the right to live in our own homes without being confronted by others drinking."

Rick used several other arguments, and felt quite confident in himself as he sat down.

Then the Master of Ceremonies got up. "Now, you have heard from each of the classes. Do you have any comments or questions you would like to ask anyone on the committee?"

There was that momentary embarrassed silence while everyone waited for everyone else to speak. Then someone in the back stood up.

"I just want to ask the last speaker if he really believes what he is saying?"

There was a hush over the audience, and the Master of Ceremonies turned to Rick with a puzzled face. "That's an unusual question, but I guess any question is fair play. How about it, Rick?"

"Well, sure, I wouldn't be saying it if I didn't mean it," he said. He was a little hesitant, since he wasn't expecting that question.

"Does that answer your questions?" the leader asked the one who had posed the question.

"No, not exactly. If what he says is true, then what's with this story in tonight's paper?" he said, holding up a copy of the local daily.

Rick felt his face beginning to flush. His eyes met

Wayne's and Rick could see panic in them.

"What story?" the leader asked.

"A headline here reads, '*FOUR STUDENTS ARRESTED IN RAID ON APARTMENT.*' And the article goes on to say, 'Four freshman students from Southern State were arrested Saturday night at an apartment at 205 E. Fifth St., for illegal consumption of beer by minors. All four were detained for the night, and were then released Sunday morning pending a hearing in City Court next Friday. Those arrested were: Rick Erickson, 19 . . .'"

A hush fell over the audience, and all eyes were upon Rick. He glanced around to see where there might be a door through which he could make an exit. He looked around for Kandi in hopes that she would support him, but she was nowhere to be seen.

After a pause, Rick stood up and went to the mike. "Yes, I was at the apartment, and I was arrested, but I was not drinking. In fact, I was invited to that party specifically to get some material for this rally . . ."

There were chuckles of disbelief in the audience.

"If you don't believe me, just ask someone who was at the party."

The chuckles turned to laughter, and Rick looked frantically around the room for someone to come to his defense. When no one spoke up, he said, "I'm sorry if you don't believe me. It's the truth." He stepped off the stage and headed for the door.

As he started down the dimly lighted hall, the Exit sign seemed to beckon him. Exit! That's what he wanted to do! He wanted to exit, not only from the building, but from the evening, from school, and maybe even from life. The nearer he got to the door, the faster he walked, and by the time he opened the door, he was almost running.

He began running across the grass which separated the building from the parking lot. There was a well-worn path which cut across this way, a shortcut used by many students. He found his car in the shadows. Somehow, it looked very good to him. It was one last symbol of home and his old life. He unlocked the door, and slipped into the driver's seat.

Automatically, he started the motor, and headed out of the parking lot. He had no plans, no immediate goal. He just wanted to get away from school, and away from the past four weeks.

He drove down the hill into town, and started south on Front Street, but he wanted to get out of there as soon as possible. There were too many lights, too many possibilities of seeing someone he knew, and right now, he didn't want to talk to anyone.

Again, as if by instinct, he drove through the business district, and along the road that led to the grassy lane along the river. It was the most secluded spot he knew, and since it was Monday, he was sure there would be no parties there that night.

His mind went back to the first time he had been on this road. This is where it had all begun. If he hadn't been on this road four weeks before, things might be entirely different tonight. Four weeks! How could so many things have happened in four weeks? His whole life had changed in such a short time!

He drove as far as he could, and turned off the motor and the lights. He slid down and rested his head on the back of the seat. From this position, he could see the full October moon as it was shining above the treetops and onto the hood of his car. It highlighted everything with a soft, beautiful, but eerie light. Everything was quiet now except for the sound of the water moving swiftly over the rocks in the river below.

He ran his hand across the seat toward his right, as if expecting to find a warm hand and body there, but the cold plastic seat covers reminded him that he was alone—very much alone tonight.

13 Where is Home?

When Rick awoke, his arm and one hand were asleep, and his neck hurt. He really hadn't planned on spending the night in the front seat of his car, but then there had been a lot of unplanned things in his life recently.

He got out of the car and stretched. The sun was already up, and it was evident that it was going to be a beautiful, warm fall day. He realized that he was hungry, and remembered that he had not eaten any dinner before going to the rally. After doing a few knee bends to get the circulation going, he got into the car and started to back out to the main road.

He still had no definite plans, but he had to go somewhere, and he wasn't ready to go back to school. As he turned onto the highway, he spotted a truck stop, so decided to pull in and get something to eat.

After washing his hands, and combing his hair in

the men's room, he seated himself in a corner booth. This morning, he wanted very much to be left alone. He needed to think, but every time he tried it, he could hear again the laughing of the crowd, and feel that empty sick feeling in his stomach. He could see them still sitting there, laughing, and waiting for him to return.

He checked his wallet, and found that he still had a ten dollar bill, so he ordered a full breakfast of eggs, bacon, and pancakes. At least he was going to start this day on a full stomach.

And there was his date in court Friday that he had to worry about. He knew the police had told the dean about it, and he wondered if they had also phoned his parents. If so, he had some explaining to do. It hurt him to think that he might be causing them to worry, especially when they had never really had to worry about him before.

He finished his second cup of coffee slowly, still trying to come up with some plan for the day. The idea of going back to the dorm was repulsive to him, but the thought of trying to explain the past two days to his parents was frightening. Finally, without making any definite decision, he went to the counter and paid the bill. It seemed to him that even the waitress was looking at him as if to say, "There's that phony kid who preaches against liquor, but spends his nights at beer parties."

He got back in the car and headed toward town. First, he drove the full length of town toward the North and turned into the parking lot of the *Kitchen*. He thought of having another cup of coffee, but remembered that this was where he first met Kandi, and today he was trying to forget her. Then he drove the full length South, and ended up again at the entrance to the river road. For want of anything else to do, he turned in.

Rick got out of the car, and walked through the thick grass toward the stream which was still about 20 yards away. He could hear the sound of the water as it moved swiftly over the protruding rocks. A meadowlark called from a nearby bush, and in the far distance, he could hear the sound of a truck shifting gears as it began its ascent out of the valley.

He reached the river bank, and looked down into the water. It was almost six feet down to where the stream ran, so he sat down, and hung his feet over the edge of the bank. As he did so, he looked down, and realized that he wasn't alone. Directly below, well hidden from anyone walking along the bank, sat a boy who looked to be about ten years of age. He was just sitting on the narrow sandy ledge next to the water, and staring into it. Because of the sound of the running water, he had not heard Rick.

After Rick watched him for a few minutes, he said, "Hi, there, fellow."

The boy, suddenly brought back to reality, turned around with a start. "Oh, Hi—you scared me."

"Say, aren't you supposed to be in school?" Rick asked.

"You ain't no cop, are you?" the boy asked with a frightened look on his face.

"No, nothing like that. I'm just a student from the college—or rather, I guess I should say, I *was* a student. Come to think of it, I guess I'm truant too," Rick said, laughing.

"You a truant?" the boy said, his eyes getting bigger. "How often do you do this?"

"First time for me," Rick said. "How about you?"

"Aw, I do it a lot," the boy said, almost bragging. "Never been caught yet. Say, if we're both truant, why don't you come on down here and play. It's a good place to hide from the officers."

"O.K.," Rick said, jumping down beside the boy. "What'll we play?"

Suddenly Rick felt light-hearted. The boy's little freckled face and broad grin somehow made him feel very young again.

"Well, sometimes I play that there's somebody drowning out there, and I swim out and try to save him," the boy said, pointing to the stream.

"Isn't that a little dangerous? Does your mother know about this?"

"Oh, no. If she ever found out, she would kill me. She doesn't know much of what I do. She works nights, and is always asleep when I leave in the morning, and she's gone to work when I get home from school. She makes me go home for lunch so that she can at least see me. She never has time to go to school to ask about me ... so whenever it's a nice day, and I don't feel like studying, I come down here and play." Then, without catching a breath, "Say, what's your name?"

"Rick. What's yours?"

"I'm Mike. Michael Judson Hale. Come on, Rick, take off your shoes. The sand is warm, and besides, then we can play in the water. I'll bet you can't catch me without getting wet!"

Mike started to run toward the water. "Come on," he cried with boyish glee.

Rick took off his shoes and socks, and rolled up his pants legs, and started to chase Mike. Suddenly, Rick was no longer a college student with some hard decisions to make. He was a little boy again playing barefoot in the sand. He and Mike ran and laughed. Sometimes he caught Mike, and then they dropped on the sand, and Rick would pin him down until he would give up, but as soon as Rick let him up, it would start all over again. Once Rick slipped and dropped full length in the water. When he got up and brushed his wet hair out of his eyes, Mike was standing on the shore, doubled up with laughter.

Rick came out of the water, and sat down on the sand. "O.K., I give up," he said, totally out of breath. "It has been too long since I've done this sort of thing, and I need to rest a minute."

Mike immediately dropped down on the sand beside him, and pushed his little body very close. They both sat there breathing very hard, and just staring into the water. Finally Mike broke the silence. He turned serious eyes toward Rick and said, "Rick, what are you going to be when you get out of school?"

"Why such a big question all of a sudden?"

"Well, people keep asking me as if I'm supposed to know," the boy said. "How do I know what I want to do?"

"Well, Mike, I'll have to admit to you that I don't know what I'm going to do any more than you do. I once thought I knew, but right now, I'm not sure."

"I've thought about being a policeman, or a fireman, but our teacher took us to the firehouse the other day, and it looks kinda scary to me. Maybe I'll just be a jet pilot," Mike said, with an air of finality.

"You probably won't understand a thing I'm going to say," Rick said, putting his arm around the small frame beside him, "but I want to tell you something."

Mike laid his perspiring head against Rick's wet sleeve. He was obviously hungry for this kind of attention and love.

"We all make dreams . . . lots of dreams," Rick began. "When I was your age, I dreamed about being just about everything I ever saw and about being like everyone I ever met. Then one day I met a man who was really cool. He was kind and good and went around visiting people, and on Sunday he got up and preached a sermon."

"Oh, I know who you mean. He was a priest," Mike said.

"Well, we called him our pastor," Rick answered.

"Anyway, one day after I heard him preach, I decided I wanted to be just like him. So I talked to him about it after church was over. My parents waited for me in the car, and he took me into his study, and we talked some more about it, and then he prayed, and I prayed, and I told God that I wanted to be a preacher. My parents were very happy, and told everyone about it. I got up in a meeting soon after that and told lots of people about my decision, and they all told me afterward how nice it all was. Then for a number of years I told everybody I was going to be a preacher, and they, too, would smile, and say, "How nice."

Rick felt the little body relax and he knew that soon Mike wouldn't be hearing a word he was saying, but he didn't care. He had started talking now, and it made him feel good. It was good to talk to someone who wouldn't make value judgments on what he was saying . . . even if he were asleep.

He began to talk about camp and fireside services, and testimony meetings at church. He talked about Ann, and how much he thought he loved her. He started to talk about Kandi, but his words frightened him, so he became silent.

In the silence, he seemed to sense the presence of God . . . just like he had sensed His presence at campfire services, so he began to talk to God. By now he knew that Mike was asleep, so he talked freely.

"Lord, I know You're here. I can feel You very close to me. I don't know why You should be close, 'cause I've done a lot of things recently that You probably don't like. But I want You to know that I do love You, and I don't doubt for a minute that You love me. I don't understand why I do the things I do sometimes, nor why I think the things I do, but somehow I believe You understand. I really want to do Your will. Will You please help me out of this mess I'm in, and tell me what You want me to do?"

How long they sat there, Rick didn't know, but he suddenly realized that the sun was high in the sky, and that his stomach was telling him it was past lunch time. "Say, Mike," he said, shaking the boy, "aren't you supposed to be home for lunch?"

Mike sat up and rubbed his eyes. "What time is it?"

"Don't know. Don't have my watch, but it looks like it must be past noon."

Mike was wide awake now. He jumped up and grabbed his cap, and started scampering up the bank. Halfway up, he stopped and turned around. "Say, Rick, I want to hear the rest of your story someday."

"Sure, Mike, someday I'll tell you exactly what I want to be, but right now you had better go home."

"Say, Rick, aren't you going home?"

Rick thought for a minute, and then got up. "Sure, Mike, I'm going home," and then he added, "wherever that is."

He picked up his shoes and socks and began to climb the bank after Mike. On the way up, he picked Mike up and began to run toward his car, both of them laughing all the way.

"Come on, Mike, we're both going home. I'll give you a lift."

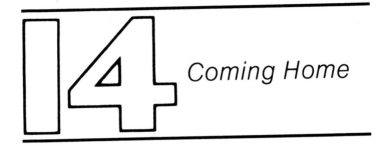

Coming Home

Mike wouldn't let Rick take him all the way home. By walking the last couple of blocks, Mike could make his mother believe he was just coming from school, and it also gave him time to think of some excuse why he was late.

Rick was thinking clearer now, and he knew that sooner or later he would have to face the kids at school again, so he decided he might just as well do it now. With that decision out of the way, he headed back toward the campus.

He parked in the lot behind the dorm, but decided to go around and enter by the front door. The thought of going through the same door he had exited by brought back too many memories.

As he passed the information desk, he noticed mail in his box, so he stopped to pick it up. There were three letters: one from his mother, another from Ann, and one was an intra-office envelope from some department at the college. He decided to wait and open the letters when he got to his room. As he walked through the lounge, he shuffled the envelopes in his hands, trying to imagine what each one contained.

It was the middle of the afternoon, so there were very few students around. Most of them were either in class or working, but out of the corner of his eye, he saw a lone form uncurl itself from one of the big chairs and come toward him.

"Not you again!" Rick exclaimed in disbelief. "What are you up to this time?"

"I'm waiting for you," Kandi said softly.

"That sounds familiar. How did you know when I would come back?"

"I didn't."

"How long have you been waiting?"

"Since early this morning," Kandi replied.

Rick continued to stare. "But why?" he asked.

"I needed to talk to you," she replied.

"It seems to me that most of my problems are the result of having talked to you," Rick said.

The hurt look on her face made Rick wish he hadn't said that. Her eyes were red from crying, and she looked as if she could start again any minute.

"O.K., I'm sorry," Rick said. "But you really didn't expect me to have a nice friendly chat with you as if nothing had happened."

"I wouldn't blame you if you hated me," she said.

"I've considered it!"

"Can't we just sit down and talk?" Kandi pleaded, taking hold of his arm.

As she began to lead Rick back to the corner of the lounge, he saw for the first time that she wasn't alone.

"Randy, are you involved in this too?" Rick asked.

"You're the one who introduced us. Remember?" Randy said.

"I'm sorry I got you involved, and I'm sorry about last night. I'm sure it was a big letdown for you and the other guys."

"That's O.K.," Randy said. "Kandi explained it all to me, so I know it really wasn't your fault. I'm sure the others will understand too."

"I still don't see the reason for this reception committee," Rick said, sitting down across from Randy and Kandi.

"You really didn't expect us not to wonder about you, did you?" Randy asked.

Rick realized that in all of the turmoil of the past night, he never once thought about anybody looking for him, or even wondering where he was.

"No, I didn't think anyone cared that much about me—especially after the way I goofed up."

"Well, we did, and some of the guys were out all night looking for you," Randy replied. "I'm here because Kandi wanted to talk to you, and I thought she needed some support."

"I've done a lot of thinking since Saturday night," Kandi began.

"That makes two of us," Rick replied.

"I'm sorry for what happened," Kandi said, tears beginning to form in her eyes.

"If you're talking about Saturday night," Rick said,

147

"I'm the one who decided to go to your party. Nobody forced me."

Rick looked over to see Randy's reaction.

"I'll leave if you want me to," Randy said, "but Kandi has pretty well filled me in."

"Stick around," Rick said. "I think we both need your help and advice."

"Saturday night was only part of what I did to you. You see, when you got scared and left me that very first night, it was a big blow to my ego. Nobody had ever run out on me before, and I had to get back at you someway. First I lied to Bert and Marcia about our relationship because I couldn't admit defeat."

"But you admitted to Bert that you lied."

"Only after Bert convinced me that he didn't believe my story. He said, that after living with you, he was convinced that you had too many principles to do such a thing."

"I guess I've blown that confidence," Rick remarked.

"Bert doesn't know anything about the party. You see he and Marcia were picked up that night for possession of drugs and they are still in jail."

"That's why they searched my room," Rick said.

"And my apartment," Kandi added. "They had me down to the police sation most of yesterday for questioning because they found some marijuana in our bedroom. I didn't know it was there—honest."

"I wondered why you weren't at the rally."

"I didn't get home until about 8 o'clock, but Randy told me what happened, and I'm sorry about that too. You see, I invited you to that party to embarrass you. I even tipped off the police that a party was going on there."

"I guess I never knew how far a woman would go to get even. But why are you telling me all of this now? You've had your fun, and now if you'll just stay out of my life, I'll try to make some sense out of it again."

"She's trying to say she's sorry," Randy broke in. "Do you think she would have waited here all day for you if she didn't mean it?"

"Why this sudden change of heart?" Rick asked, still sounding skeptical.

"When I finally got home from the police station, I was really bummed out. So many things had happened so fast, and I was alone, and I began to think—really think. I began to ask myself where I was going, and what purpose I had in life—just like we talked about that first Saturday morning. All I knew was that I had to talk to someone. I called the dorm, but you weren't in, so I called for Randy. I knew he believed like you do because I had talked to him several times in the Union. He came over last night, and we spent most of the night talking."

"Did it help?"

"He showed me where I could get help. He showed me some verses from his Bible, and for the first time that I can remember, I prayed. Really prayed." She paused. "Rick, I don't know much about being a Christian, but I really want to learn."

"I'm sorry that I was such poor help to you," Rick countered. "I was trying to fit into your world instead of introducing you to mine."

"Now will you forgive me for what I have done to

149

you?" Kandi said.

Rick stood up. His first impulse was to take Kandi into his arms and say, "Yes, I forgive you. Will you forgive me?" But he noticed Ann's letter still crumpled in his hand, and somehow it didn't seem right to be holding Kandi and Ann's letter at the same time.

So instead, he looked down to where she was sitting and said, "Kandi, you know I forgive you, and I need to ask for your forgiveness too. I certainly didn't make a very good Christian example for you to follow. You'd better let Randy help you, he's got his head screwed on straight."

Randy and Kandi both stood up. "Thanks for all your help, Randy," Rick said. "I think Kandi needs some rest. How about taking her home?"

"Yeah, I'll take her, and you'd better get cleaned up. You look like you've been swimming with your clothes on."

"I have," Rick said, but he knew Randy didn't believe it, and he wasn't about to explain.

Randy left with Kandi, and Rick started up the stairs to his room. For the first time since coming to college he felt things beginning to fall into place in his life. He still had a lot of unresolved questions in his mind, but at least there was no longer any question about the reality of God. He knew God existed, and was actively involved in his life.

When Rick opened the door of his room, he saw immediately that Bert's side was empty. He opened Bert's closet. It was empty. He looked in the drawers, but they too, were empty, and his desk, which had been cluttered since the first day of school, was clean. Rick saw a note on his desk, so he picked it up and read:

To Bert's Roommate:

As you probably know, Bert got himself in a little trouble, so we are taking him home with us. He probably won't be back this quarter. Hope we didn't take anything that belonged to you.

Mr. and Mrs. Kemp

Rick had not really developed a close relationship with Bert, but as he looked around the empty room, he felt lonely and sad. It seemed as if he were responsible, in some way, for Bert's problems. If only he had been a better witness to Bert, maybe things would have been different.

He was still holding the three letters in his hand. By now they were getting wrinkled, and even a little soiled from his perspiring hands. He knew, deep inside, that each one could contain another piece of the puzzle of his life, and he was afraid to check where that piece might fit.

He decided to open his mother's letter first—that one seemed less threatening. He did expect her to be unhappy about Saturday, but she was usually quite understanding. The letter was filled, as usual, with family news, and contained only one mention of Saturday. The last sentence read: "Sorry you found it necessary to leave so soon on Saturday.

We will be looking forward to your coming in two weeks, and we will plan to spend the day with you."

Rick breathed a sigh of relief as he laid down that letter, and picked up the intra-campus envelope. He assumed it was from the dean concerning his court appearance. Instead, it contained the following note:

Dear Rick:

You may have noticed that I was at the rally on Monday night. After the accusations were made against you, I decided to investigate for myself. I couldn't believe you had changed that rapidly. So, I talked to some of the students who had been at your party, and I found out that your story was for real. I took these students to the police station, and after giving their testimony, the police have dropped all charges against you.

Hope you don't mind my meddling in your affairs.

Gerald A. Leonard

Rick re-read the note. He couldn't believe that a professor would be that concerned about him. He was deeply moved, and a little embarrassed that he had caused Dr. Leonard this trouble. Rick had always been led to believe that Christians were the only ones who loved their neighbors. He began to compare Leonard's concern for him with his concern for Bert, and he realized that he had been so concerned about himself that he had had little concern for either Bert or Kandi—at least not a concern that was coupled with action.

There was one letter still unopened. Maybe this one would make up for all of the hurts of the past few days. Opening Ann's letter made him feel like he was going home—if not in reality, at least in heart. He took his time, trying to make the most of each moment. Then he began to read:

Dear Rick:

I'm sorry I was gone when you came home this weekend, but maybe it was for the best. You see, I had the opportunity over the weekend to do a lot of thinking about our relationship last summer. I have begun to wonder how much of it was the result of a very special time and place, and how much of it was real love. Now that we are away from camp, and away from each other, things look different to me. How about you? I wish we could sit down and talk about it.

Maybe we should each try going with someone else for a while, and see what happens. I'm sure there are lots of girls at Southern who you could date, and some of the guys at church have been asking me to go out.

I'm sorry if this hurts you, but you had to know how I felt. Let's talk about it the next time you come home.

Love,
Ann

Rick let the letter drop out of his hands, and sat staring at the wall. If this had happened two weeks earlier, he would have probably gone into a rage and jumped into his car and headed for the Cities, but now it was different. He had been through a crash course in life, and he was better equipped to handle crisis situations. He felt a mixture of sadness and relief, but most of all, he was at peace with himself.

He walked over to his bed, kicked off his shoes, and laid down with his arms under his head. He was staring at the ceiling when the door opened and Randy came in.

"Hi," Rick said, "back already?"

"Yeah, I just dropped her off. She needed some sleep."

"Don't we all," Rick said, without taking his eyes off the ceiling.

"Are you all right?" Randy asked, sitting on Bert's empty bed.

"I was just thinking."

"About what?"

"About how one can never really go home again after you've left."

"I know what you mean, but it works both ways."

"How's that?" Rick asked.

"When you go home, you're not the same fellow who left either."

"Never thought about that," Rick said.

"No, we can't go home again, but we can always take some of home with us wherever we go. After eighteen years in a Christian home and community, we can't just suddenly switch worlds. We bring Christ, and our Christian training into our new world, and it isn't until we integrate the two that we find happiness. Our background affects everything we do and say, and every decision we make."

"Randy."

"Yes."

"Are you going to help Kandi?"

"I could, but she really wants you," Randy answered.

"Did she say so?"

"Only in a thousand ways."

"Really?"

"Your name was in every other sentence last night. She may have started out by trying to get even with you, but in the process she has fallen in love."

"With me or Christ?" Rick asked.

"With your help, it can be both," Randy answered.

ABOUT THE AUTHOR

"In twenty years of college teaching," says Ed Groenhoff, I observed firsthand what happens to some of our Christian kids when they leave home for the first time."

He believes that a novel like *The Freshman* is an excellent opportunity for teens to live vicariously through some experiences (including the solution to problems) before they actually meet them.

"This book takes a Christian kid through the first quarter in state college and attempts to show how he faces the problems of sex, drugs and humanism in the context of his Christian perspective."

ED GROENHOFF is presently Executive Director of Communications for the Evangelical Free Church of America, based in Minneapolis, Minnesota.

His other books include:
Psalms for Cloudy Days
So You're Going to College
The Quiet Prince
It's Your Choice
Jerry's Summer

Boyd County Public Library